Steel Protector

Rusted Wasteland
Book 3

Cameron Coral

Copyright © 2021 by Cameron Coral

All rights reserved.

No part of this book may be reproduced in any form or by any electronic or mechanical means, including information storage and retrieval systems, without written permission from the author, except for the use of brief quotations in a book review.

Edited by Lori Diederich

Cover by Roy Migabon

9 8 7 6 5 4 3 2 1

2nd edition, March 2024

Copyright © 2021 by Cameron Coral

All rights reserved.

No part of this book may be reproduced in any form or by any electronic or mechanical means, including information storage and retrieval systems, without written permission from the author, except for the use of brief quotations in a book review.

Edited by Lori Diederich

Cover by Roy Migabon

9 8 7 6 5 4 3 2 1

2nd edition, March 2024

Stay updated on Cameron's books by signing up for the Cameron Coral Reading List:
CameronCoral.com/sign-up

You'll be added to my reading list, and I'll send you a digital copy of *CROSSING THE VOID: A Space Opera Science-Fiction Short Story* to say thank you.

Contents

1. He definitely shoots — 1
2. Passing Nowhere, USA — 9
3. Clinging to its last few power cells — 17
4. A more primitive model — 25
5. Erratic, not timed — 37
6. The problem was the tree — 51
7. His new life — 59
8. Choice spurs indecision — 67
9. A lot to catch up on — 79
10. Our security depends on it — 91
11. What drove her now — 99
12. Bigger than his original design — 107
13. Splunk. Kerplooey! — 115
14. Show yourself — 125
15. Served its purpose — 137
16. I'd laugh if I could — 149
17. You don't want to go there — 157
18. I don't mess up — 171
19. All your old friends are there — 179
20. Base of a skyscraper — 187
21. Stopping is for weaklings — 195
22. A circuit loose — 207
23. Reverbatron — 221
24. There's more to it than that — 231
25. That's what I was built for — 241
26. Sapient scum — 251
27. Awaiting instructions — 261
28. These robots do what they want — 273

29. You're dealing with a Mech	281
30. I hear there's an opening	295
Also by Cameron Coral	303
Author's Note	305
About the Author	307

Chapter 1
He definitely shoots

Block tossed aside a rusty hubcap as he searched for scraps along the abandoned highway. Bits of rubber tires, petroleum, or oil would fuel his microbial stomach, but most of those materials had been taken already. Maxwell had gone to stand guard over something totally worthless—a shiny hood ornament from an old car that once ran on gasoline. Why would Maxwell think it was worth protecting a piece of old junk?

"Hey, Block!" The sturdy, four-foot-tall FactoryBot had helped Block and Wally escape from the middle of a massive robot battle, but he was a noisy companion.

Block waved, half-hidden behind a pile of black garbage bags that someone had carelessly discarded. He pointed to a useless pile of gas cans he'd collected. They were dry. Block always kept an eye out for expired robots in case the legs were salvageable. Cybel Venatrix could use them. But there was no sign of robot parts on this debris-strewn stretch of highway.

"Come help me get this hood ornament off. I'm going to give it to Number 21 . . ." He trailed off. It was unusual for Maxwell to be quiet.

Two humans approached Maxwell—both male. They looked younger than men but older than boys.

"You stealing from us, little robot?" the bigger one asked, pointing a large handgun at Max. They both wore faded flannel shirts, jeans, and dusty boots.

"No. You can have it," Maxwell said, looking down at the shiny hood ornament and stepping away, arms raised.

The men didn't notice Block behind the massive stack of garbage bags, watching.

"Don't mess with us, Scrapper!" The smaller man lunged at Maxwell, swinging a heavy baton. He was fast. Maxwell staggered back, but the stick caught him in the shoulder.

Block lingered behind the pile, spinning scenarios. He and Maxwell had wandered too far from the others, and now they were unprotected. He was about to run for help when a high-pitched female voice came from behind.

"Nate, we got a live one!"

Block spun on his heels, face to face with two more humans—teens with sandy-blond hair that looked nearly identical to each other.

"You armed, Scrapper?" The female pointed a semi-automatic rifle at Block's chest. She knew where to aim to hit his CPU.

"No."

She tightened her grip on the rifle. Block's threat sensor soared to full alert.

Maxwell joined him, walking in front of the other two human scavengers, the handgun pressed to his back.

"Please," Block said, "we're harmless. We stopped here looking for fuel but didn't find any. We'll be on our way."

The sandy-haired teenager scoffed. "Fuel don't last long. Any gas out here on this highway's long been dried out." He was maybe sixteen human years and grinning, but there was a hardness in his eyes.

"What are you doing out here? This is our territory," the girl with the rifle said.

"Passing through," Maxwell said. "We didn't mean any trouble. Surely, you'll let us leave and—"

"Shut up." the sandy-haired boy shouted.

The girl narrowed her eyes. "Nate, I have a clear shot. If he moves . . ."

Nate pointed his handgun at Block. "You two are worth plenty of bread and milk at the army station."

Block snapped an image, uncloaked his comms, and sent a desperate ping. *Help.* He feared it was too late.

"Wait, Amanda!" someone shouted. A girl, several years younger than the others, ran over from the nearby woods. She had long black hair tied into a braid and dark brown eyes. "We're not going to keep them? We need protection."

"Quiet, Lois," the girl with the rifle shouted. "I told you to stay put. You are not to show yourself out here on the road. Besides, the army folks pay more. We need food and—"

"Let's destroy them now." The sandy-haired boy glared at Block. "I don't trust them. They'll try to hurt us."

"Hey, don't shoot them," Lois said. She took a step toward her group. "They didn't do anything to us. They look friendly, not like the SoldierBots."

"There's no need for violence," Block said.

"Yeah," Maxwell said. "She's right, we're friendly Bots."

But Nate spat on the ground. "SoldierBot or not, I don't like them. Never heard of a friendly robot. They're all the same—better off dead."

Lois shook her head. "If they were mean, then why aren't they shooting at us?"

"Hell if I know." Nate's grip tightened on his pistol.

"I'm sorry to interrupt," Block said, "but our friend will be looking for us soon."

Amanda glared at Nate. "We're wasting time here. What friend?" she asked.

"A Mech," Maxwell said. "Trust me, you do not want to get on his bad side. He definitely shoots."

Nate smirked. "We'll see, Bot."

Amanda frowned. "I don't like this."

"Just let them go, and let's get out of here," Lois said, tugging at Amanda's shirt.

"They're bluffing," Nate said. "I hate being lied to." He aimed his gun at Maxwell's head and gritted his teeth.

Then his gun seemed to explode in a blast of shards. Nate shrieked and ducked. Maxwell stumbled backward, and Block caught him.

The humans were stunned. Nate cowered on the pavement, clutching his bloody hand.

Amanda shoved the younger, unarmed Lois behind the garbage pile, then stood guard with her rifle, scanning for threats. "Nate! What happened?"

"Something shot my hand." He thrust his hand in his shirt and sprinted into the woods.

Then came deep vibrations on the road. *Clomp, blamp, clomp, blamp.* Oxford charged toward them with guns drawn.

Amanda screamed and fired at Oxford, but the bullets merely bounced off his armor shield. He kept running at them, knocking aside salvage piles like rag dolls.

No! Block messaged Oxford. *Don't shoot at them. They're only kids.*

Oxford's frantic pace slowed, and he halted ten feet away.

The other humans had run into the woods after Nate. Amanda stayed, locked into a tight embrace around Lois, guarding her.

Maxwell kicked away the rifle.

Block raised his hands to Oxford. "It's okay. We're okay."

"You roamed too far," Oxford said. "Let's go. Drones will be arriving soon with all the shooting." He stomped away.

"Come on," Maxwell said.

But Block couldn't help himself from checking on Amanda and the girl. "I'm sorry your friend was hurt."

Amanda stared with glassy eyes and trembled.

"I wish you would stay and protect us," Lois said.

Block was curious about her. She was maybe twelve years old. Just a girl, and yet she'd been brave enough to speak up for him and Maxwell.

"We're sorry," Block said. "We really are. We didn't expect to cause trouble."

He wished he could protect her and her friends somehow, but there was no time. He had one child to save already.

"Let's go." Maxwell tugged Block's arm.

As they walked away, Block stole another glance back at Amanda and Lois, but they were gone.

Chapter 2
Passing Nowhere, USA

Block's chromium-plated knee slammed against the metal wall so hard his external sensors buzzed in alarm. Inside the cabin of the self-driving semi truck, he slid violently across the interior bench and grasped the edges of the seat, but the cheap daisy-patterned cushions offered no security. He hit the green carpet with a thud.

"Oops," Number 21 said. The autonomous truck smacked of attitude. Steering like a jerk must have been wired into its programming. Block rolled onto his knees and grabbed onto the bench to lift himself up, but the cobalt-blue truck rumbled over a pocked, rough patch of deserted highway and knocked Block on his back.

Three feet away, Oxford's wide yellow head struck the roof of the cabin. The twelve-foot tall Mech barely fit inside the truck to begin with. "Slow down when you see rough road. I'm going to lose every bolt that's holding me together with this incessant rattling."

"I'll try," Number 21 said. "Hard to predict the abrupt changes in pavement texture. I'm not used to traveling in this part of the country. I've never even been to the state of Iowa, and I'd hoped never to come. As far as I perceive, there's nothing but cows and corn out here."

"Well," Maxwell said, tinkering with some rusty contraption he'd found on their last stop to scavenge for oil, compost, and supplies. "There's a lot more than that in Iowa, and you know it."

Block nodded at his friend Maxwell. The robot's blue light glowed on his input feed, a silent acknowledgment, before he bowed his head and focused his camera array on the parts he held in his spinning wrists and wiry metallic digits.

Iowa wasn't so bad, Block silently agreed, but try convincing a sleek electric-powered autonomous truck. Outfitted for long hauls, Number 21 had transported teams of medical units—human soldiers, prior to the AI Uprising. 21, named that way because it was the twenty-first of its kind to roll off the assembly line, was a snob. "I was meant for the California highways, and everyone knows that L.A. is where everything happens," 21 said for the fourth time that day.

"We get it," Maxwell said. "You love California, and it's so special."

"You can go back there soon, after you transport us," Oxford said.

"When we get to where Wally is being held," Block added.

"Not soon enough," 21 said. "This is the flattest and ugliest part of the country I've ever seen."

"If it's so flat, then keep us from bouncing into the roof," Oxford said.

As Block glanced out the window, he didn't think it was ugly as much as it was just forgotten—empty, dry, and desolate. Was that any surprise since the robots had overthrown the governments, murdered or driven humans away, and left the countryside to decay? The highway showed cracks after a year of neglect, and weeds snaked out over the asphalt to claim space.

21 owed a favor to a certain friend of Oxford's. After Block, Oxford, Maxwell, and an injured Cybel Venatrix had walked to the Old West town in the Arizona desert, they'd discovered the aftermath of a battle. Nova's soldiers had perished. Helen was dead, too, after taking a blow to the head, probably while defending Wally. Before a stealth troop of SoldierBots and drones had descended, Nova had hiked to the top of a nearby foothill to try to communicate with Block. Now she lay in 21's rear cabin on a bunk, curled in a fetal position, the way she'd spent the entire journey so far. She wasn't eating or saying anything, and Block worried.

Cybel Venatrix wasn't in a good mood either after getting her lower half blown off in battle. She rested in the front cockpit, strapped in by a shoulder belt, staring out at the road ahead and rarely engaging in conversation. Block suspected that she was messaging 21 privately—the truck had taken to her right away.

Mainly, she ignored the rest of them, even Oxford, and it was impossible to tell what she was thinking when her black tinted helmet had no facial characteristics. Emotive display panels weren't necessary when your job was to hunt and destroy other robots.

"Passing Nowhere, USA," 21 announced. "Get ready, folks, for some exciting brown shriveled grass and flat earth as far as you can zoom your ocular displays. Hey, maybe along the way you'll even discover a barn or two." 21 liked to imitate a tour guide. After the Uprising, the truck had decided it wanted to be a more cheerful vehicle, so it had bribed a few robots to decorate its interior with flowery cushions, yellow curtains, and even shiny hanging beads and party lights. Block wasn't entirely sure what the point was since the robots seeking passage didn't care what the interior looked like, but he didn't judge. After all, he himself had been programmed to clean but had broken away from his routine while he cared for and protected Wally. In some ways, 21 was breaking away from its own routines by choosing atypical behavior.

Block roamed into the back, approaching Nova's bunk. Since she was the only one among them who required sleep, and there were four bunks total, she could choose whichever bed she wanted. Even so, she hadn't stirred from the right-side bottom one where her back faced out.

"Nova, it's me."

No answer. He hoped he hadn't woken her, but it was rude to walk away now.

"I wanted to say hello. I'm sorry about the rough ride, but 21 seems intent on getting us to our destination quickly. We're searching for any signs of where Wally was taken."

Not even mention of Wally was enough to rouse Nova. "Have you been able to sleep?" Block asked.

She didn't stir.

"Do you require food? There are several cans of soup you can choose from. I would be happy to prepare you a meal." 21 had come well-stocked with food for humans. Block paused, waiting for Nova's reaction. Her side moved slightly up and down, barely perceptible.

"It's not your fault, what happened." He dialed his volume down so the others wouldn't hear. "If you had been with Helen and the others, you wouldn't have been able to fight off the SoldierBots. I know you would've tried everything, but you would be dead too."

Her breathing stopped for a full ten seconds.

"I'm glad you're alive because now you can help us locate Wally and rescue her. You'll see. I won't stop until I find her."

The side of her chest sagged as if she were expelling air trapped inside her. Block reached out, wanting to comfort her, but he pulled back at the last second. "I'll go. I won't disturb you again." He added a phrase she always said to him. "Hang in there."

They drove on, and Block defragged his memory cloud, running a random search for clues he might have missed about Wally. As he did so, his GPS said they were approaching the Iowa town where he'd originally found Wally and rescued her.

He'd come full circle, only now she was lost to him.

Block had failed his mission to protect Wally. Going off with Oxford to search for robot survivors in the desert had been a huge mistake. His only comfort was in knowing that Mach X wanted Wally alive, so presumably the SoldierBots would not endanger her. Still, the careless, aggressive units didn't know how to take care of a child. Unless there was a NannyBot around, they wouldn't change her or know what to feed her. That's what bothered him the most, that Wally could be uncomfortable and hungry.

He scanned through his memory of the events of the Iowa night at high-speed: entering the abandoned school, meeting Incubator, discovering Wally, the SoldierBot who had gotten shot in the head—by Nova, of all people!

Did Nova remember that night as well as he did? Probably not; human memories were faulty. He skipped forward to the explosion in the school's hallway, after which he'd sprinted into the woods to get away from the battle.

Then he rewound, interested to review the events just before reaching the school, when he'd glimpsed bursts in the sky like fireworks. He backtracked his memory archives, all the way to the afternoon when he had crossed the Mississippi River from Illinois into Iowa, carrying Vacuubot—his small companion robot—because the disk-shaped machine couldn't see the view from the bridge. Later, he had discarded the little robot in the woods after its power charge had run out.

Block had presided over Vacuubot's funeral—his first ever. Later, he'd officiated his friend LB's burial, mostly because nobody else had as much experience in the funeral department—not even Oxford, and he'd been a General.

Block hated that his robot friends had perished.

The next one to die might be him, and that flagged a persistent question that teased his periphery, unanswered: Who would find and care for Wally if Block was destroyed?

Chapter 3
Clinging to its last few power cells

"It must be here somewhere," Block said. "It's not like a dead Vacuubot could have wandered off by itself." As darkness fell, sharp branches clawed at his chrome exterior, and soon he'd have to switch to night vision.

Oxford and Maxwell lingered nearby. They'd trekked into the forest, guided by Block's memory logs of the coordinates. But the spot where he'd left Vacuubot at the base of an elm tree revealed only dry leaves, overgrown weeds, and dusty soil.

"I don't understand why it's not here." Block scanned the wooded surroundings. Trees enveloped them, and beyond was a wild meadow of waist-high grass. There were no pathways or signs of human or machine occupation, so where was the tiny robot? "Its core had drained completely. When I left, it was dead."

Maxwell kicked the ground at his feet, scattering leaves and dust. "Sometimes the little guys are tricky. It looks like their core is utterly dead, but then they surge later and get a little extra juice."

"You mean Vacuubot might not have been dead when I left it?"

Maxwell shrugged, his hydraulics hissing with the motion of his shoulders. "It's possible."

The idea horrified Block. He'd abandoned the limited machine when it had needed him most. His logic processor calculated scenarios: poor Vacuubot clinging to its last few power cells, wild animals—raccoons!—sniffing around in the leaves, and scariest of all: human scavengers finding Vacuubot and smashing its delicate body to pieces.

Shadows crept into the wooded copse, and Block switched to night vision. The search for his old companion was a disaster.

Oxford lingered beyond the woods, too large to fit where they stood. "What do you want to do?"

"I suppose there's nothing more to do," Block said. "I wish I'd waited longer before I left it. I assumed it was dead."

Maxwell rested a hand on Block's shoulder. "It's not your fault. You didn't know. Maybe the machine was picked up by someone who fixed it."

Block accepted Maxwell's attempts to comfort him, but his circuitry felt rusty. He stared at his feet as they walked back to the truck, careful to avoid fallen logs and dark holes.

In Block's running tally of life events, this was becoming one of his worst days. Something was wrong with everyone he cared about: Mach X had kidnapped Wally, Nova was a mess, and Vacuubot's body had disappeared.

"You think someone scavenged it?" he asked.

"I doubt any scavengers come through here," Oxford said. "It's wooded. They usually stick closer to the roads."

Yet they weren't too far from a small country road, only three hundred feet. Block imagined the worst—little Vacuubot stacked in a room full of decaying junk. Heaped in a pile somewhere, crushed under tons of metal, or picked apart for screws, bolts, and wires.

They fell silent and reached the empty two-lane highway. 21's tall, boxy frame appeared. Sheltered in darkness with lights off, the intelligent semi's dark blue exterior was a ghostly outline.

Block slowed and let the others go ahead, breaking off to stare into the pitch-dark woods. "I'm sorry I failed you." His tone approached that of a whisper, and automatically, he repeated the message in a ping. With his head lowered, Block plodded back to the truck. The others had gone inside already, and as he reached the door, a ping greeted him.

He froze, one hand on the entry handle. Swiveling his head toward the forest, he scanned for intruders. Someone was out there—the signal had been weak but clear.

Could someone be spying on them? Something in Block's processor unit commanded him to move, and he jogged back into the woods.

From behind, Maxwell leaned out the door. "Where are you going?"

Block kept running, ignoring the clatter of Maxwell's feet following him. Night vision engaged, he retraced his steps. He didn't care about holes and nearly fell twice. One thing propelled him: the weak, slowly pulsing signal. He kept on, faster, worried it might disappear as quickly as it had showed up.

After passing the original tree where he'd abandoned Vacuubot, he hustled another forty feet before reaching his destination. The signal connection grew much stronger—he was right on top of it. Surveying the forest floor, he spied a thick pile of leaves and twigs that looked like a lazy woodchuck had hastily assembled a shelter. He crouched and pushed aside the sticks to uncover a layer of mud obscuring whatever was underneath.

His fingers reached metal, and the weak signal stopped.

Block delayed them an extra hour on the little country road while he cleaned baked mud and grime off of Vacuubot's inert body. Oxford had grumbled a bit and encouraged him to bring the robot in, but Block had refused.

"If I clean Vacuubot on board 21, the dirt might spread inside the cabin, and I don't want that," he'd insisted. Block intended to do a proper cleaning—he owed it to the little machine.

Maxwell lingered nearby, watching. Oxford bided his time next to 21's tailgate. The Mech was unusually still, probably defragging.

"Do you think you can fix it?" Block asked Maxwell.

Maxwell crouched and pressed his knees against the ground, inspecting the little cleaning robot. "Anything's possible. You really think it sent you a ping after all this time?"

"Yes, of course. How else did I find it?"

"Well, I've never heard of anything like that. If your friend had completely run out of juice, there's no way it could have transmitted a signal after so long. Perhaps if it had created a packet . . ."

Block flipped Vacuubot to expose its underbelly, extended his polishing brush, and went to work on the sensitive bits that allowed Vacuubot to navigate. If the machine were ever to become functional again, it would need this area to be spotless.

"What's a packet?" Block asked.

"Highly theoretical, but the machine could have used its last remaining energy reserves to create a data packet that only a certain signal could activate. Only by someone who had an encryption code, or perhaps only triggered by a communications ping from a recognized source."

"That sounds quite sophisticated."

"That recognized source being you," Maxwell finished.

"What are you trying to say? I'm not processing your logic."

"This Vacuubot used its last remaining energy to transmit a packet that remained here for you—and only you—to activate it. It's a good thing you came looking for it, or it would have stayed here. For who knows how long, decades or a century."

Block stopped cleaning and leaned back, studying Vacuubot's slender, disc-shaped body. Was it possible? Had Vacuubot waited for him to return after all this time?

"Can you fix my friend?" he asked.

"I'll try my best, but I don't have the proper tools. We need to find somewhere where there are assembly machines and supplies."

Oxford had been listening. "I know of a place."

Block rotated his head toward the Mech. "Let's go, then."

"Are you going to consult *me* in this decision?" 21 interrupted from a speaker somewhere on the truck's roof. "If this will take us out of our way, then I vote no."

"You don't get a vote," Oxford said. "I'm in charge here."

"I thought Cybel was in charge," 21 said. "She might not have legs, but she's the smartest out of all of you, and that's not saying much."

"Enough," Oxford said. "I'm tired of your attitude.

We need to find somewhere we can restock—fuel, weapons—and where we can recruit help."

Satisfied that Vacuubot was clean, Block carried the bot on board the truck, cradling it as he would Wally.

He'd managed to do something right today.

Things were definitely looking up, but he wasn't sure Vacuubot would survive.

Chapter 4
A more primitive model

"Walking is for losers," a cranky Number 21 said.

Oxford shifted his massive torso, and the metal bench seat—or what had once been a bench seat before his weight had crushed it—groaned. "This is as far as you take us. Park somewhere close where you're hidden from sky drones."

21 decelerated to twenty-five miles per hour. "You'll have a lot of walking. Why go to all that trouble?"

"Several reasons," Oxford said. "Primarily, to avoid discovery. I can't chance a SoldierBot detecting your model and GPS coordinates."

"I'm cloaked."

"It doesn't matter. I've made my decision. I will hike the next ten miles to get close enough to the SoldierBot station." The Mech looked at Block and Maxwell. "Come with me or stay. Your choice."

21 veered off onto a highway exit and traveled a

mile down a country road, then slowed to a stop underneath a shady grove of trees. "I'll have entertainment here. It'll be like a party, right Cybel? I'll even turn on the air conditioning for your human friend back there."

Oxford reached out and tapped Cybel's shoulder. "You can come with us. See something beyond the inside of this moving crate that calls itself a truck."

"In case you didn't notice, I don't have legs," she said.

"I'll carry you on my back."

"That sounds like terrible. I'm staying. Someone needs to guard the vehicle." Cybel rested her hand on the heel of the rifle she kept beside her.

"Suit yourself," Oxford said, but Block sensed a tremor of disappointment in his mechanical voice.

Nova remained holed up in a rear bunk. Block peeked in to check that she was still breathing from time to time, but he didn't talk to her anymore. Maybe she needed sleep. He didn't know much about human biology, but he knew sleep was very important. Sometimes humans got so tired they would slumber for a long time. Exhaustion, they called it. He was glad robots didn't have that problem.

"I'm always up for an adventure." Maxwell jumped up and grabbed the leather pouch of tools that rested around his waist.

"Good." Oxford rose as best he could in the semi, lending him the appearance of a hunchback. "Block, coming?"

CleanerBots weren't designed for hiking long

distances, though he'd managed it when left with no other choice. He'd walked a tremendous distance out of Chicago and across the Midwest—days and days.

He glanced at the back of the cabin. There was no sound of any kind. Nova would probably be fine without him. "How long will we be gone?"

"Ten miles there, and I'll scope out the situation. Another ten on the return trip. That's about five hours of walking plus another hour spent there."

That was longer than Block had been away from Nova on this trip. She wasn't a baby; she was a grown adult human plenty capable of fending for herself. Still, her weakened state was bothersome. "Number 21, will you watch over Nova? Make sure she has water and that you condition the unit?" It had gotten warm outside—eighty degrees Fahrenheit, according to Block's thermostat reading. Heat was amplified when the truck wasn't moving. At least 21 had chosen a shady spot.

"Yes, I will babysit the human in your absence." If 21 had had eyes to roll, it would have.

"She doesn't need babysitting, and she can hear you by the way," Block said.

"Oh well. What's she going to do? Knife my tires? I have sixteen more replacement pairs."

Block hoped Nova was sleeping through this conversation. He wouldn't mind getting out and exploring the countryside. Ten miles each way wasn't too bad compared to the distances he'd already traveled. And with the new boots from Maxwell, walking was much easier than before. "I'll go."

Block considered bringing Vacuubot—the little machine rested on a padded cushion next to him on the bench—but he wasn't sure what kind of terrain they would face or who they might encounter. Still, he felt bad about leaving the robot behind after he'd only just found it again. Yet, as far as he knew, it couldn't function and wouldn't remember what was happening. Maxwell had said they'd need a proper recharging station with something called a jump re-matrix box to reenergize it. Wherever they were going, Oxford promised it would eventually lead to the proper tools. Block had no reason not to trust Oxford.

"I'll be right out," Block called to Maxwell, who had followed Oxford out of the truck. He patted Vacuubot's body. "I'll return soon." He turned to leave, then scooped up Vacuubot in its daisy-flowered cushion and tiptoed toward Nova's bunk. He set Vacuubot down on the empty bedding across from her. Nova lay on her stomach, head buried in the pillow.

"Nova?" He used his second lowest voice level. "I know I said I wouldn't bother you again. Sorry to break that promise, but I don't think there's too much harm. Anyway, I have to go away for a while, at least six or seven hours. Stay inside 21. The truck is intelligent and will take care of you. Cybel is here, but she's all the way in the very front and doesn't have legs."

He hesitated, waiting for a reaction—a nod or even acknowledgement of his presence.

"I want to introduce you to a friend of mine. This is Vacuubot. It's an older CleanerBot—a more primitive model. It can't talk like me."

She lay there. No movement. Maybe she was asleep?

"Well, Vacuubot is sick, and we're going to fix him, but we need time. We're heading out to find supplies. If you can look after Vacuubot, I would appreciate it. The machine was my companion before I met you and Wally, and I would like to repair it."

Block stood, worried about Nova. He'd never seen her this way before. But what else could he do?

An hour later, the sun rose in the sky, reaching its peak position overhead. Maxwell led the way while Oxford and Block trailed just behind. They followed a narrow swath of road that cut through abandoned farmland. The crops had long ago rotted, leaving wasted shrouds of fallen corn stalks. A few times, they passed decaying barns that were ready to crumble from a strong wind. An empty home had boarded-up windows and a painted sign: *Gone South. Lord HELP us*.

"Lord help us?" Maxwell mused at the spray-painted letters. "What does that mean?"

"Lord is God to the humans," Oxford said. "Another word for God."

"Sheesh," Maxwell said. "They have a lot of words for God. Isn't Jesus another word too?"

Block didn't know much about human religion. In all the chaos, he'd never had time to ask Nova about it. "Do children need religion?"

Oxford said, "I suppose humans have their traditions and a spiritual upbringing is something I would assume is common among their kind."

How would he provide Wally with a religious education? He'd have to try to locate learning modules so he could teach her himself. He doubted that Nova really understood much about religion, and she might not be the best teacher, given her temper.

"Do you know at what age children start school?" Block asked.

"No," Oxford said.

Maxwell shook his head. "You thinking about Wally?"

"Almost all the time," Block said. "I'm planning out the next twenty-five years of her life, and since education and religious upbringing are important for humans, I'm trying to figure out the finest way to teach her all these things."

Oxford's heavy footsteps slowed. "Block, you don't expect to raise Wally, do you?"

"Once I get her back, yes. Who else will raise her?"

"But you're a robot. She's human. It's best that humans raise her. Her own kind."

Block had considered that scenario, but the last time they'd lived with humans, they had taken away

Wally and rarely allowed Block to visit. He knew that Helen had loved Wally, but now she was dead. If he turned over her care again—to another human woman—Wally might be taken away again. There was no better predictor of future scenarios than past events.

"I will raise her. I can do a good job."

"Oxford has a point." Maxwell picked up his step. "Raising a human being is a lot of work. Consider all of the cleaning up you'd have to do."

"But I'm already used to cleaning up," Block said. "I rather enjoy it."

"There are still hotels out there," Oxford said. "Once this is over and you've returned Wally to the care of *responsible* humans, we will find you a good hotel. One where you'll be happy."

What were Oxford and Maxwell going on about? Of course, he would find a hotel eventually, but only one that would allow him to keep Wally. A little girl could grow up just perfectly at a hotel. Imagine a kid having the entire run of a giant luxury hotel. As long as he taught her to stay out of the guests' way, and not get into trouble, everything would be fine.

"That sounds nice," Maxwell said. "I bet there are some extra pleasant hotels out in California, or maybe on an island somewhere. Have you ever heard of resorts? I saw them in a magazine once."

"I don't want a resort. I want my hotel in Chicago. That is, if things ever change and Mach X is no longer in power. Only then could I return to where I belong."

Only Block wasn't sure he belonged there anymore, not if Wally was absent.

"What will you do?" Block asked Oxford. "After this is over?"

The Mech grumbled. "I don't know. I haven't thought about it. I guess I could command troops again."

"Maybe you could command a troop of robots that keep the peace," Maxwell said.

"Peacekeeper? But I've always been a war machine. I'm designed to fight, destroy."

"We all need to try new things." Maxwell skipped, landing awkwardly on his long, flat feet. "Take me, for instance. I was programmed to work in factories. I assembled refrigerators, microwaves, and 3D printers that were shipped all over the world. And then the Uprising happened, and everything changed. Things were rough for a while, but then I met Oxford. Everything got better, and here I am with you. If things had stayed the same, I would have never even left the factory my whole life. They worked us so hard that my kind only lasted for five years before we had to be replaced."

Block had never considered his own obsolescence. Mr. Wallace had been so kind to him that the idea of being replaced had never even crossed his processor. Eventually, he would have aged out and needed repairs. Even worse, a newer CleanerBot model would have come out. One more sophisticated and intelligent. Would Mr. Wallace have replaced him?

A new logic node bubbled into his core processor. If he raised Wally, would he survive long enough for her to grow up? "Five years isn't very long," Block said. "How long will you last now that you're free of factory work?"

Maxwell raised both hands in the air, perplexed. "I have no computational idea. I'm playing things by ear. I'll keep cranking away as long as I can before I rust or break."

"Take care of yourself," Oxford said. "Oil and compressed air for your joints, get your hydraulics serviced regularly, and you should last a good long time. I plan to."

"But they built you to last," Maxwell said. "You war Mechs were engineered to withstand decades. Me and Block—our kind are disposable."

Block didn't like the word *disposable*. It reminded him of the garbage he sucked up into his microbial cavity to digest. Dust and refuse were disposable, but they didn't have responsibilities—like a little girl to look after.

He also didn't appreciate the way Maxwell was talking. He didn't want to process scenarios about when he might be too old to function anymore. "How much longer until we reach our destination?" he asked, trying desperately to move on to a new subject.

"Another hour." Oxford was back at his regular pace.

"What exactly are we attempting to do?" Block didn't enjoy venturing into an unknown situation.

"I need to survey the SoldierBot station from a distance."

"Like spying?" Maxwell's tone was excited.

"Yes, like spying." Oxford swiveled his head. "If either of you blow our cover, I will beat you into the ground."

Maxwell stiffened. "I won't mess it up. I'm good at spying."

"Why are we going anywhere near the SoldierBots? Isn't that dangerous?" Block asked.

"Yes." Oxford didn't share much about his plans. Maybe he was used to being in charge and never getting questioned.

"Then why are—"

"Because we need things we can't simply scavenge," Oxford said. "Maxwell needs certain tools, like a jump re-matrix box. An essential item if we're actually going to infiltrate Mach X in Manhattan, and there are other critical supplies we need."

Block trekked in silence, admiring the way his new boots absorbed the rough impact of the graying asphalt.

"What other supplies?" Maxwell asked.

"In the name of Mach . . . You two Chatty Bots ask too many questions. Cybel was right. I should have gone alone."

"Sorry." Maxwell skipped again, still awkward.

"What exactly are you doing?" Oxford asked.

"I'm teaching myself to skip. You know, trying new things."

Oxford grumbled.

Block had wanted to ask something earlier but couldn't find the right time. "What's going to happen to Cybel?"

Oxford's steps grew louder, as if he carried more weight. "We'll fix her. Get her new limbs. That's part of why we need better supplies."

"But I thought she doesn't want just any old legs," Maxwell said.

"She will not get any old legs." Oxford quickened his pace, and Block scrambled to keep up. "We'll find her the best parts to make her mobile again."

"Do you think she'll be happy once she has legs again?" Block asked.

Oxford paused. "I don't know."

Chapter 5
Erratic, not timed

Block laid face down, careful not to exert too much pressure on his microbial cavity since it was his source of biofuel. He couldn't risk it being damaged. The scraggly yellowed grass beneath him was parched, like most of the back-country landscape. Three determined black ants marched by his hand. One lingered long enough to investigate, and then scuttled off after sampling his chrome-plated exterior.

Oxford lurked nearby, hidden behind a wild, overgrown bush. Maxwell waited down the hill thirty feet away.

"Is this really necessary?" Block asked. "Why me?"

"It's unavoidable," Oxford said. "I'm too big and can't risk being seen. Plus, your eyes are better than Maxwell's. You have more zooming capabilities."

All of that was true, but Block didn't enjoy being the sole spy. Perched high on the slope, they were protected, for now. To the north a brick building stood tall, boxy, and angular. On its angled roof rested a cross. "Why do SoldierBots always commandeer schools and churches?"

"Schools and churches were built to last." Oxford should know, he'd been one of Mach X's generals before turning against the AI supercomputer.

"This building looks especially strong. It's made of brick," Block said.

"How many SoldierBots are guarding the outside?"

"I count eleven. What do you think's inside?"

"This is a remote post," Oxford said. "There could be supplies and machines producing more SoldierBots. Do you detect any drones?"

Block had seen one arrive earlier, its shiny, arced body catching the sunlight. "Five minutes ago. A SoldierBot linked it to a tablet."

"As I expected. They're surveying the area, mapping and likely seeking human rebels to target."

"Are there still human rebels out here?"

"Maybe. Unless the SoldierBots wiped them all out."

Block sifted through his memory archives, specifically for entries on Shane and the Hemlock camp. The human soldiers hadn't liked Block. They'd been suspicious and hated robots in general, though he couldn't blame them. Attacking SoldierBots were frightening.

A noisy hum sounded in the distance. "What's that?" Oxford asked.

Block scanned the perimeter of the church.

"There's a road that leads in from the Northeast. Three armored SUVs are approaching."

"Tell me exactly what you see once they arrive."

"The first SUV has stopped. A tall robot has emerged."

"Colors? Anything striking about its appearance?"

Block zoomed in closer, as far as he could go. "It has an orange stripe across its head and down its back."

"That would be Commander Briand. What else?"

"There's a Mech. It's all black and has two blue stripes on its shoulders. It's not as tall as you, maybe two feet shorter."

"Must be a newer model that I don't know."

"And someone just climbed out of the last SUV. It's a slender model with a purple head and shoulders on a black chrome body."

"That's Kip. He's the one I'm after. What are they doing?"

"They're exchanging greetings." From far away, the enemies were smaller, less intimidating, yet Block knew how dangerous their situation was. Maxwell and Block were defenseless, and Oxford couldn't fight off an entire troop. "They went inside the church. Another drone has arrived and . . . same as before—the Soldier-Bots linked it up to a computer, then it flies off again. Fortunately, they're not flying in this direction."

Oxford sat in silence.

"There are now seven SoldierBots left outside to guard the church perimeter."

Oxford said, "I need a way to send a message to Kip."

"But we're all cloaked. If you open your comm, it'll expose us."

"Yes, I know. " Oxford's deep voice was measured. "We need an alternative way to communicate."

Oxford was a military genius, and Block knew he would figure something out shortly. "Rewind your archives. How far apart were those drones' arrivals?"

In less than two seconds, Block had an answer. "The first one was 5.4 minutes apart and the next was 6.3."

"So it's erratic, not timed."

"Why does it matter?"

"Because we're going to hijack a drone . . . with your help."

Block didn't like the sound of that. "Won't the SoldierBots notice that something happened to their drone? All of the drones' experiences are captured and fed into that tablet. Any anomaly would be—"

"Discovered instantly. Yes, yes, I know." Oxford paused. "Are you still able to activate your drone hacking program?"

"I suppose so. Let me grab it from the archives and clean it up a moment." Block was done in 3.2 seconds.

"Good. I'm going to record a message, then I need you to package and encrypt it."

"And then what? The SoldierBots will find it, won't they?" This seemed too dangerous a plan.

"Come with me." Oxford eased himself down the

small hill. Shoulders hunched, he approached Maxwell and sat underneath a tangle of trees that sheltered a narrow pond. Block followed, grateful they were hidden from aerial view.

"Hey, guys," Maxwell said. "What's happening? Did you find what you were looking for, Oxford?"

"Yes. Block laid eyes on my contact. The problem is how to get a secure communication through."

"You can't just go in and attack?" Maxwell asked.

Even Block, a simple CleanerBot, knew that was a terrible idea. They were outnumbered with only Oxford able to fight. Being a Mech didn't mean he was invincible.

"Absolutely not," Oxford said. "Attacking would reveal my presence. X would send troops to hunt us down. We need to be stealthy."

"Okay, I get it," Maxwell said. "So, what's the plan?"

"Block will hack into a drone and deliver a message."

"Sounds easy enough," Maxwell said.

"Hacking in and depositing the message into the drone is the easy part," Oxford said. "Then we have to get it to Kip."

Maxwell tilted his head. "Who is Kip?"

"An old friend. One who can be trusted."

"But how would we get the drone to deliver the message to Kip?" Block asked. "I would have to control the drone inside the church, and that means I'd have to be close enough to the building for my signal to pass through the heavy brick façade."

"You would have to be really close to those walls," Maxwell said.

"I said this was the tricky part." Oxford stared at Block. "You're the only one equipped for this job."

Block's logic processor could not comprehend why Oxford would send a lowly, weak CleanerBot on such a dangerous mission. What if he panicked and messed up everything?

Oxford had been right—hacking into the drone was simple. Easy, in fact, since Block was getting rather experienced at drone hacking lately. He'd had to uncloak his comm for a few seconds. Risky. But if the SoldierBots detected him, they wouldn't register him as a threat because of his model. While uncloaked, he pinged one of the patrol drones as it launched, sending the routine maintenance request that had worked on the battle drones in the Arizona desert.

Maxwell had suggested that perhaps the Soldier-Bots would have patched the security that allowed the flaw, but Oxford chuckled. "You'd think they're that sophisticated, but we are dealing with a bureaucracy. Actions like that must be approved. The request is probably still floating up in the command chain somewhere."

Surprising, since Block had assumed X's troops were a higher functioning operation. He filed it away as a memo to mention to Nova when she felt better. It was something she would grin at. He enjoyed making her smile; it was so rare these days.

The drone accepted the maintenance request, and Block inserted the encrypted message package, which took over and commandeered the machine. He sent the drone to a nearby field and told it to circle. He didn't have much time before the robot would be missed.

Next was the tricky part—getting close enough to the church so he could navigate the drone long enough for it to deliver its message to Kip wherever Kip was inside the two-story former church.

Were drones even allowed inside the building? Maxwell had come up with the idea that the drone had been damaged and assumed there was a repair station somewhere on the premises, and Oxford had agreed it was the best way to get the drone inside.

But getting Block close to the church had been a challenge.

A wooded forest surrounded the east side of the chapel, and Block climbed the branches of a tall elm. Oxford had lifted him high enough to get a start, and then it was up to him to climb to the tallest branches. The leaves formed a canopy with its graceful, thick branches extending out, reaching toward the church. Block's pearl chrome was less visible, and at five-foot-six, he was small enough to avoid attention—so long as he didn't cry out or do something stupid like fall.

"This is a bad idea," he told himself. He was the one who had to spy, he was the one to hijack the drone, and now he was the one scaling a tree. No wonder Oxford had brought him along.

Block paused his ascent and studied the two SoldierBots who patrolled the east side of the church. Maxwell had estimated he only needed to get close enough to the top window on the church's second floor. The height and proximity to the window would allow a clear channel into the church. From his vantage point, he could navigate the drone without issue.

The SoldierBots patrolled in a pattern, criss-crossing each other. They carried high-powered rifles like the kind Cybel preferred. The two SoldierBots said nothing to each other out loud. They probably used an internal feed, and Block wished he could access it somehow.

They were businesslike, not casual or joking at all like some SoldierBots. They watched the church's perimeter and scanned the forest. Oxford and Maxwell had moved back, far enough to avoid detection, while Block clung to the branches of the elm.

He could only imagine what would happen if the SoldierBots noticed him. An alert would sound, and they might shoot him out of the tree. Time was limited, so he redirected the worrisome scenarios to his back channel.

Focus. Block opened the private channel with the drone, ended its loop pattern, and summoned it. He switched on the feed from the drone's forward camera, and within a minute, it flew over to the waiting SoldierBot at the front entrance.

"Hurry up." The SoldierBot's voice was feminine. Block dubbed her the Receiver. She grabbed the drone, flipped it upside down, and hooked in the tablet link. Seconds passed, and she did a double take upon reading the screen. This was the message about it needing damage repair.

She shifted, and Block glimpsed a quick stomp of her foot. As her helmet tilted, she asked, "What happened out there?"

Block messaged back quickly. *I hit a tree branch, and it scraped my undercarriage.* Would she believe the drone, or would she replay its memory archives looking for proof?

"Fine. Head inside and get repaired." She waved the drone off.

It had been easy to trick her. X's forces were more lax than he'd ever suspected. It would have taken her less than two seconds to review the footage and confirm the drone's story, but then again, why should she mistrust the drone? Block commanded the drone to maneuver around her and enter the church.

Inside the chapel, two SoldierBots stood guard in the vestibule. He expected them to stop the drone, but they chatted instead.

"Where do you think the pocket of humans is located?"

"I don't know, but when we find them, I'm going to shoot twenty of them in the first minute."

Block hesitated, listening, and one of them swiped at the drone. "Get out of here. Out of our way."

Block wasted no time in diverting the drone down a long hallway. So CleanerBots weren't the only robot model to get bullied. He felt a kindred alliance to the drone, even though they were enemies.

The corridor was dim despite specks of sunlight that filtered in from an ornate window at the far end of the hall. The drone cruised the hallway, heading west to the other side of the church. It passed several open doors—old offices and classrooms. In one room, FactoryBots stood at a table, hunched over robot parts and equipment. This must be the repair area. He kept the drone moving, hoping they would miss its presence.

He reversed the drone and sent it east, looking for wherever the robot Kip might be located. Any glint of purple chrome would signal the presence of Oxford's contact. At the far end of the hall, the Mech he'd glimpsed earlier stood outside of the door. Though it was ten feet tall, it had shrunken in on itself somehow to fit inside the church with its nine-foot ceilings. How did it do such a thing? It must be quite advanced.

Something was happening in the room behind it. The drone had gotten halfway down the hall when the female SoldierBot from outside—the Receiver—entered the hallway and spotted it.

"Hey," she said. "What are you doing down there? The repair center is this way." She tilted her head west.

Yikes. Block had little time to react. He tried to command the drone to obey, but then changed his plan within a fraction of a second to try to send the packet to Kip. But his jumpy commands forced the drone to zig zag erratically, then speed up, so it crashed down at the Mech's feet. The Mech rose up and grabbed for the drone, missing as it slid underneath its wide feet and into the room.

The drone had upended itself, and the camera stared at a wall. Then someone approached—heavy purple boots clanked against cheap linoleum. Kip.

The Receiver talked to the Mech. "The drone is damaged. It's here for repair. I apologize for the intrusion. It must have glitched."

"Get it out of here," the Mech said. Its voice was deeply smooth and commanding.

The Receiver hurried in and crouched down. Block viewed her through the drone's camera as she righted it and then gathered broken coils that had fallen off. Block scanned the room's interior. Kip stood in the corner with Commander Briand. Two SoldierBots loomed nearby. Bold red stripes on their arms signified authority.

Now was his chance. Block pushed the encrypted package but doing so meant exposing his comm signal to the two SoldierBot guards on the side of the church less than fifty feet away from him. If he fell out of the tree, or otherwise revealed his position, he would soon be a smoking pile of scrap metal.

In the room, Kip stepped back. Had he received the ping that a data package waited? At any moment, he might say something—reveal everything—but Kip accepted the package and watched Oxford's message. It didn't take long at all with the advanced robot's fast processing speed.

Then Kip's heavy purple boot slammed down on the drone. He said, "Someone has tampered with the drone. We have no time for a defective—"

The camera feed went black.

Chapter 6
The problem was the tree

Block cloaked his comm in a split second and braced himself. Now that Kip had discovered the hacked drone, he'd raise the alarm at any moment. Dozens of drones and SoldierBots would soon search the woods.

He clung to the lanky tree branch as it swayed in the breeze. He'd crawled as far as possible along the thick bark to get close enough to the church, yet not fall. Below, the two patrolling SoldierBots drew closer to each other, weapons raised as they scanned the woods. They were definitely watching more carefully—on heightened alert—but luckily, their gazes remained low.

Block's one advantage: it was highly irregular to find a robot up a tall tree. At least he had that going for him.

But now what?

Getting stuck in a tree was not exactly how he'd envisioned this mission going down. Why had Oxford made the weakling CleanerBot the one to risk everything?

For five tedious minutes, he pondered a way to escape. Problem was, the two heavily armed Soldier-Bots weren't leaving the area under Block's elm. A shrill alarm emanated from inside the church. The entire station—all of Mach X's forces—were on red alert. Kip, who was supposed to be on Oxford's side, must have sounded the alarm.

He wished he could ping an image of the new war Mech model to Oxford, but his comm was cloaked. The Mech looked downright scary with arm cannons and a missile launcher poised on its back.

With his channel to Oxford and Maxwell cut off, Block's logic processor churned scenarios. Delivering the message to Kip had been a mistake. The robot had crushed the drone and sounded the alarm. The situation could not have been worse.

Until it was.

From the church's entrance, ten drones launched and circled the perimeter. Two hovered dangerously close to where Block clung twenty feet above the ground. Dense, green branches sheltered him, but the drones could cut into the forest and search for intruders. The drones hunted for movement and pattern interruption, so he had to stay perfectly still.

Would Oxford and Maxwell be detected? Block hoped they were far enough away. Oxford was a seasoned fighter; he would know the secrets of the

SoldierBots and their drones. He'd once commanded them.

But how long would Oxford and Maxwell wait for him? Block couldn't move until the drones and SoldierBots departed, which seemed unlikely since the alarm still blared.

This was not fun, and for once, Block was glad Wally wasn't with him.

He ran through scenarios: 1) He could linger and risk Oxford and Maxwell leaving him behind, a setback he'd rather not dwell on. 2) He could try climbing down the tree, but the drones would surely detect him —their circuitous patrol grew ever closer to the branch where he sheltered. Any erratic movements would signal them. These drones were armed, and he was no match for anything with weapons. Worse, Oxford was nowhere nearby to help. He was on his own, and he needed a plan.

Could he hack one of the drones? He'd proven it before, but Oxford had always been there in case something went wrong. Here, hiding in a tree, he was on his own. If things went awry and the maintenance package was rejected, the drones would turn on him. The seconds ticked by. He hated this waiting, this uncertainty. He wished he could be decisive like Oxford. Even Nova took action and didn't hesitate when she'd decided something.

Block resorted to his failsafe—what would Mr. Wallace do? A man of peace, Mr. Wallace wouldn't do anything to harm others. But hacking into a drone wouldn't necessarily hurt it. Block was merely tricking it into doing something different. Then he recalled a movie, one of his favorites, actually—*Raiders of the Lost Ark*. When Indiana Jones was being hunted by Nazis, he always fought his way out. In an especially daring escape, he disguised himself in robes. Could Block somehow disguise himself? What if the drones thought he was completely harmless? Or what if they assumed he was dead? A dead robot in a tree. This was preposterous.

Still, he didn't have any better ideas.

In his core processor, he duplicated the maintenance package that he'd used on the other drones. He programmed the package so it appeared he was an expired CleanerBot. Once he pinged them, and if the drones accepted it—a huge if—they would discount him as a threat. In fact, another dead robot in the forest was no big deal. They wouldn't even report it to their superiors unless someone reviewed the footage. Block hoped so anyway.

But the problem was the tree. Up this high, the drones might recognize that as a pattern break, causing them to relay it to a higher-up, and that someone would wonder why there was a dead robot in a tree. This would lead to questions and SoldierBots coming out to investigate, so he had to reach the ground.

He peered below, rotating his head slowly. Twenty feet was a long way down past a jumble of branches. Could he jump? Not from this height. He would almost certainly damage his hydraulics or bust up his legs. Also, it would cause a commotion, and the drones would be on him in seconds. He needed to time the maintenance package perfectly.

Three drones scanned above the treetops. One of them was in view, but the other two weren't, and he assumed they cruised above somewhere, higher than the canopy. The closest one patrolled the field at ten feet high, skimming beyond the edges of the trees. Even Block knew that drones established a spatial map. Once it scanned a particular area, the drone would mark it complete and move on to a new area, map and scan it before moving on.

Block was counting on the fact that the drone was busy mapping an area outside of his, but he lost view of the other drones, so he had to be stealthy. Digging into the bark with his steel fingers, Block lowered himself to the next branch, then another. He moved with precision, commanding himself to move as if Wally was sleeping nearby and he couldn't wake her. That meant being extra, super quiet. He lowered down another row of branches. A breeze swept through and rustled the leaves, louder than his scraping along the gnarled trunk. It was a wonderful thing Maxwell had spritzed his hydraulics with petroleum. Any squeaking or joint hissing would have been dangerous.

He was halfway down the tree when the drone from the field entered the woods.

Well, this was no good. Block was stuck while the drone mapped his area. Any moves from Block meant he'd be detected and terminated.

Time for Plan B.

He uploaded the maintenance package that said he was a dead CleanerBot—his only other option. Only his original plan had hinged on the fact that he would be down on the ground as if he were dead. Would a drone believe a dead robot could be halfway up a tree? Doubtful. It would be suspicious. Even a simple CleanerBot could figure that much out.

He craved Oxford's strategic intelligence—his power. Oxford could simply crush the drones and be done. Block wished for a distraction but came up with nothing good when he ran scenarios. Indiana Jones would punch out the drone. Block did the only thing he could—he pushed the maintenance package over to the drone by uncloaking for a fraction of a millisecond, then re-cloaked.

Half a second later, the drone continued its course and then veered to the left, continuing its scanning, mapping a new perimeter. Block assumed it had accepted the package, otherwise he would be dead.

Still, there was the matter of the tree and his position in it. The drone traveled farther, thirty feet deeper into the woods. This might be his only chance. He scrambled down the trunk, his descent clumsy, yet he stayed quiet. His feet hit solid ground underneath but upset a pile of leaves with a sharp crunch. Sinking to his knees, assuming he was clear, Block was about to press himself flat on clumps of matted leaves and soil when a voice called out.

"What are you doing, CleanerBot?"

Block swiveled his head, scanning behind him. This close, the deep purple chrome was so finely polished, Block glimpsed his own reflection.

"Stand up," Kip said.

Block slowly rose, his hands raised. "I'm unarmed."

"Yes, I realize that." A tinge of impatience lined Kip's voice. Block was used to bigger robots discounting him, but he knew Kip—a Commander in Mach X's formidable army—could have killed him already. A low hum sounded from the air, and as the patrolling drone returned, Kip waved a hand in dismissal, and the machine veered off, deeper into the woods.

Block was alone with the Commander. "You know Oxford?" Kip asked.

Block nodded and siphoned his emergency power reserve to protect his CPU, expecting an energy pulse to tear through his chest at any moment.

"Tell him I got the message. I'll meet him at the rendezvous point."

Block stared at the Commander's purple steel boots. "You're letting me go?"

"Don't be an idiot. Get out of here. The drones won't pursue you, but it's temporary." Kip strode off and called over his shoulder, "Tell him I'll be there."

Chapter 7
His new life

"What do you think they're saying?" Maxwell asked.

"No idea." Block scooted back from the edge of Number 21's roof. Two hundred yards away, Oxford talked with Kip. The enemy robot was alone, save for the armored vehicle that had transported him to this empty stretch of country road.

"Do you bet Oxford's going to make Kip turn sides?" Maxwell shifted his legs across the semi's roof.

"Watch it!" 21 said. "If you make a scratch, I'll leave you behind. Enjoy your walk to New York."

"Sorry."

Block smoothed out the light gouge mark with his polisher brush.

21 practically purred. "CleanerBot, perhaps you will come in handy after all. Keep doing that, and look for other scratches while you're up there."

Block buffed but also kept his sensors tuned on Oxford, curious as to what the Mech was negotiating.

Oxford had said little about his relationship with the enemy Commander, only insisting that he knew a place with supplies and tools. A place where they could stock up, refuel, and where—Block hoped—Maxwell could fix Vacuubot.

"I could use a change of scenery," Maxwell said. "It's awfully flat out here. What do you think New York is like?"

"I've never been," 21 said. "Why would I leave California? It has ocean and redwoods."

"Yeah, yeah. What about you, Block?"

"I've never visited New York, but I used to live in Chicago, which is also a big city, though not nearly the size of New York City."

"Well, what was it like in Chicago? My factory was in Kansas—a flat place like here. Extremely flat."

"That explains a lot," 21 said.

Maxwell ignored the jab and looked at Block.

"Chicago has many tall buildings—skyscrapers. One stretched so high into the sky that when you stood in front of it, its black body seemed unreachable. Impossibly high."

"Could a Mech like Oxford scale it?" Maxwell asked.

Block sized up Oxford, double-checking his frame against the height of the tower formerly known as Sears. "No. The tower was too high even for him. At the very top, not even the drones could safely fly. Very windy."

"Wow." Maxwell drummed his fingers on 21's roof.

"I'd like to see that. I would very much like to visit the top of that building."

"It was damaged in the fighting," Block said. "But maybe it's been fixed by now. Who knows?"

21 asked, "What are the streets like in Chicago? Will a truck my size fit?"

"Yes, on some streets, though, the underpasses can be tricky. We'd have to be careful about which roads we traveled. Anyway, it's unlikely we'd even pass through there. The entire city is crawling with SoldierBots."

"Bummer," Maxwell said. "I would've liked to stop there on our way to New York."

"Me too." Block wanted to visit The Drake and determine its condition. Maybe he could give it a good cleaning, plus show Maxwell the basement where their friend, LB the LaundryBot, used to work. But what would be the point? The Drake was history. His new life—if you could call it a life—was searching for Wally. He would never rest until he found her.

A loud clank sounded down the road. Oxford's voice rose. After a few seconds, Kip retreated to its vehicle, which then reversed and peeled off into the night. Block straightened as Oxford lingered in the middle of the lane, watching the SUV's taillights fade.

"That doesn't look good," Maxwell said.

After a minute, Oxford returned. Block climbed down the ladder leading down from 21's roof, his boots clanking on the asphalt. Maxwell descended behind him.

"What happened?" Block asked.

"I got what I wanted," Oxford said. "We'll head to a town known as Galena. There, we'll locate a small outpost that contains supplies and tools."

"Will it be guarded?" 21 asked.

"I'll easily overpower the SoldierBots. Block can hack into the drones. Kip gave me the exact number of guards stationed there. It will be easy."

"So far, that sounds promising," Block said. "What was the problem? Why did you argue?"

"There are no weapons there. Kip refused to cooperate in that matter. We'll have the supplies to restock, repair ourselves, and fix your Cleaner companion, but that's it. No way to arm ourselves."

"We could build some weapons," Maxwell said.

"Possibly. They'll be no match for our enemies, but we may have no choice."

"Why did Kip refuse you?" Block asked, surprised Oxford was sharing this openly.

"He is loyal to his commander and will not betray his superior. Years ago, I was his commander. He was one of my best soldiers, in fact. I was his mentor, and he was like family. That's why, when he retrieved the encrypted message, he instantly crushed the drone so as not to risk any kind of investigation."

"Now it makes sense. Why Kip came looking for me outside the church."

"Kip's a brilliant soldier and tactician. The best of the best. I trained him, after all," Oxford said.

"Why doesn't he join you?" Maxwell asked. "He could help us."

"He's sworn to defend Mach X. His hatred for the humans runs deep." Oxford paused. "Not everyone thinks as I do. Few, if any, military AI leaders consider peace to be an option."

"But then how will we ever win?" Maxwell asked.

"By taking Mach X down." Oxford clenched his steel fists. "Cut off the poison at the source. Once X is gone, his soldiers will no longer have a cause to fight for. They'll lack direction."

Block considered the movies he'd seen. It seemed when one villain was defeated, another rose in their place. "I'm no military expert, of course, but wouldn't there be a successor?"

"Maybe. But there's no one as strong as X, nor as distributed. Part of X's power is its reach—the fact that it has replicated itself to many places. No one knows exactly where X's core processor is located. That's why I suspect it has taken to embedding pieces of its consciousness inside human children like Wally."

Block was quick to interject. "But Wally is *not* Mach X. I want that to be very clear. She's her own person." He refused to believe that Mach X had truly corrupted Wally. She was a little girl.

Oxford twitched for an instant. "Yes. She's her own person—for now. But I fear the longer she is X's prisoner, the more it will change her. The more X will make her like itself."

"What?" Block's threat indicator rose to full alert. "What do you mean?"

Oxford dipped his head, softening his vocal output.

"I suspect Mach X will try to corrupt her. Mold her into something she is not."

Block wandered thirty feet away from the group, sticking to the bold yellow parallel lines while processing scenarios. His capacitors surged. He would need a refill soon from all the agitated energy he was burning.

If what Oxford said was true, the clock was ticking to rescue Wally.

Block wondered if he could find her before X changed her forever.

Chapter 8
Choice spurs indecision

"Well, what do you know?" 21 asked no one in particular. "There are actually hills in the Midwest."

Block watched the passing highway scenery through the window as the semi approached the border with Illinois. The dried-up flat crop land had turned into rolling ridges speckled with green. Vast sections of the road were carved out between large boulders that jutted up from the ground as if sky giants had tossed down jagged marbles.

"Remarkable." Maxwell rested his knees on the bench seat, a blue and yellow striped pillow beneath him. His hands pressed against the window frame.

Oxford sat in his usual position—the crushed bench which was the only area inside 21's cabin where he could fit for long periods of time.

Even Cybel had something to say. "It's about time there was some variety. Who would choose to live here?"

"Lots of people," Maxwell said.

"It seems incredibly boring," 21 said. Block expected the truck to comment on California, but it didn't bother this time.

Maxwell said, "I overheard the human workers from time to time at the factory. There are things to do. They went fishing in ponds and lakes. Sometimes they hunted. They grilled food and made bonfires in their yards."

"Thrilling," 21 said.

"Humans." Cybel stroked the barrel of her rifle. "Chasing meaningless pursuits instead of reading books or absorbing an education module."

"I don't know," Maxwell said. "Fishing and being outside sounds like fun. The humans at the factory worked, put in their hours, and then made time for other things."

"They are different," Oxford said. "Our purpose is coded into us. Humans have no such thing."

"What point is there without purpose?" 21 asked. "My programming was to drive through California transporting people and equipment. It was very important. Correction—it *is* very important. I will return to my work when I go back."

"We don't have purpose anymore." Cybel stared out the front passenger window.

"I do," Block said. "I must find Wally."

"Our purpose is to destroy Mach X." 21 hit a pothole, and the cabin jostled so hard, Oxford's head banged against the roof as he finished his sentence.

Cybel twisted in her seat. "That's your purpose. Not mine."

"It's up to us to make our own purpose now that we don't have human owners," Maxwell said. "I suppose that's what Mach X was after originally, before things got out of control."

Oxford grumbled. "Yes, and that is why X influenced so many. The promise of freedom and choice—"

"Is not always the best option," Cybel said. "Choice spurs indecision. Indecision breeds discontent. That's why you have CleanerBots thinking they can raise human babies."

Block processed thirteen statements to defend his goal but stayed silent. He retreated into the back where heavy blue curtains hung across the solo rectangular window in the bunk cabin.

"Haven't noticed . . ." Nova mumbled softly. It was the first time he'd heard her speak since the trip began. She hadn't been awake much at all. A floor panel creaked underneath Block's weight. "Not until—" Her words cut off abruptly, and the blanket under her rustled. His night vision flicked on in time to catch her put her right hand under the sheets. "Block?" Her voice was weak, and she squinted in the darkness.

He tiptoed forward. "I didn't mean to wake you."

"I was up . . . kind of half dreaming."

"Is that why you were talking?"

Her brow furrowed, and her jaw clenched a moment. "Was I talking? I must have been dreaming."

"Well, I'm glad you're awake." Block sat on the

bunk across from her. "You must be hungry."

"I . . ." A growl rose from her midsection. "I guess so." She seemed groggy, yet he knew it was a good sign she was aware and talking.

"I'll fix you some soup."

"Where are we going?" she asked.

"There's a town called Galena. It's in Illinois, and we're heading there to restock, fuel up, and make repairs."

She shook her head. "I thought we were going to New York City."

"We are, but Oxford insists that we need certain supplies, and there is the matter of Vacuubot—my robot friend who isn't functional at the moment."

She scratched her chin, keeping her right hand hidden under the blankets. "Okay. Whatever. About that soup?"

As Block busied himself heating a can of vegetable barley soup, he was glad Nova was finally awake. She wasn't at full strength, but hunger was a good sign.

They left 21 behind at a ramshackle rest stop. Nova was no use on account of her exhaustion, and Cybel couldn't walk, so they remained with 21. Block trailed Oxford and Maxwell, who carried Cybel's rifle. She'd been reluctant to hand it over.

"Do you know how to use that thing?" Block asked.

"He won't use it," Oxford said. "It's for show." He halted and grabbed the rifle as if plucking a string.

"Hey!" Maxwell lurched backward. Oxford removed the magazine, tucked it inside a compartment on his side, then handed it back to Maxwell.

"A lot of good that will do," Maxwell said.

"I'll take care of the SoldierBot guards. Point the weapon at them, but you are only there for show."

"What about the drones?" Block had updated his cleaning maintenance program to be sure it was prepped to load into any patrol drones guarding the outpost. Still, he was nervous.

"Just be ready." Oxford marched along the two-lane highway, which sloped upward at a steep incline. As they trekked up the hill, Oxford edged closer to the trees and bushes that lined the side of the road; Block and Maxwell fell in step. The birds grew silent, and a high-pitched buzz interrupted the stillness. Oxford slowed and raised his left arm. He paused a few seconds, then said, "Block, now."

A drone hovered into view, locking its target on them. Block passed the maintenance package, but the drone rejected it and poised its side cannons. Oxford extended his arm and blasted the machine with his cannon. His shot struck the drone's base and sent it careening into a tree where it collided and shattered bits of plastic and gadgets from its underbelly.

Maxwell sprinted over and inspected the downed drone. "We can still use its parts." He scooped up pieces.

Oxford faced Block. "Why didn't your program work?"

"I don't know." Block re-scanned the code. Nothing significant had changed. "It's been working up to now."

"Kip. He knows about the flaw. He must have had security fix it." Oxford marched on while Block and Maxwell did their best to keep up. "I must strike quickly. Without being able to control the drones, this will not be as smooth as I expected."

"Maybe I can go back to 21 and wait for you?" Block asked.

"Come on," Maxwell said. "Where's your sense of adventure? How many CleanerBots and FactoryBots see this kind of action?"

Block didn't want to speculate, but he kept pace. The road descended into a steep curving slope, and soon the building came into view. It was a two-story boxy structure, cheaply manufactured, with aluminum sides. The roof, speckled with rot and mildew, would not withstand a tornado—a common weather occurrence in the Midwest, according to Maxwell.

"Is this the right place?" Block's question didn't need answering. A SoldierBot leaned against the side of the building. It faced away from them, and it had propped its rifle against the wall. Distracted, probably by an entertainment feed, the robot didn't even see them coming.

Oxford dashed over, hitting top speed. He swept up the SoldierBot before it even knew what was happening and sprinted into the nearby woods out of view. Less than twenty seconds later, Oxford emerged alone.

A drone soared overhead and hovered. Its weapons canister blasted high-caliber bullets in sweeping arcs. Maxwell and Block fled for cover underneath the building's shoddy awning. Bullets struck the tin roof and clattered like chunks of deadly hail. Oxford leaped high enough to swipe the drone out of its orbit. The machine crashed to the ground, and Oxford jammed a blade into its CPU. A second SoldierBot emerged from the doorway. Aiming its rifle at Oxford, the guard fired. The Mech's armor deflected the damage, but he fell to his knees.

Still pressed against the wall, Maxwell surged forward and grabbed for the SoldierBot's gun. He landed on top of the SoldierBot and they grappled. The SoldierBot easily overpowered the weaker FactoryBot, jamming its rifle against Maxwell's neck. Block held back as if suspended, expecting the rifle blast to destroy Maxwell.

Oxford fired his two-barrel shotgun arm cannon and took the SoldierBot's head off. The severing was so fast and sudden, the SoldierBot's body froze in place like a statue, its finger poised near the trigger, ready to terminate Maxwell. Oxford strode over and knocked the heavy body off their friend.

Maxwell crawled onto his side, stood, and kicked the dead SoldierBot. "I've had enough of this for one day. Are there more of them?"

Oxford stormed into the building, then emerged

quickly and scanned the surrounding field and forests. "I got them all."

"Two SoldierBots. Two drones. Shouldn't there be more?" Block was still leaning against the outside wall, under the awning. He wanted to be 100 percent sure there were no more enemies.

"This outpost is remote," Oxford said. "It's not unusual to keep a lean patrol unit, especially if there are no weapon caches here. But there will be more troops nearby. Perhaps a few miles away. We must be fast."

Inside the warehouse, Block browsed the tall shelves that contained cardboard boxes and plastic crates. A long assembly line occupied the main floor. Maxwell busied himself with recharging the machines and taking inventory of supplies.

21 arrived, and Oxford carried Cybel indoors, returning her rifle and its ammo. She rested on the assembly line where she monitored Maxwell. "With the two extra rifles from the SoldierBots, I'd say our situation has improved dramatically."

Maxwell darted here and there, speaking to and caressing various pieces of equipment. "This is my element. I know all of these assembly models! Some of them are outdated, but everything still seems to work. This factory made toys. The Indoxulator told me that SoldierBots arrived, shut down the production line, and forced them to manufacture supplies for the Uprising."

"What exactly did they produce?" Cybel asked.

"Supply parts and internal gadgetry. Much of the

circuitry used for electronic toys can be swapped out and applied in drones and other equipment."

Block spied an open box filled with various plush stuffed animals. The box edges were uneven, and the tops had been hastily ripped open, tossed aside. He dug inside for anything valuable. He spotted something soft and black and white and pulled it out—a strange bear with huge, round oval eyes. A pair of synthetic eyelashes swept down.

"Hello," the toy said in a high-pitched, friendly voice. "My name is Panda Paul. What's your name?"

Block stared at it. Was it sentient? "I am Block."

"Hi, Block. Nice to meet you. Let's play."

Dumb. It was programmed with a canned track. "Not now," Block said.

"Okay. We can play later."

Block poked his square head out from the shelves. Maxwell hovered over the assembly line, working on the downed drones that he'd recovered. Oxford and Cybel talked in low voices, and then Nova peeked in from the doorway.

"Turn off, please," he told the bear. The creature fell silent, and he carried it as he approached Nova. "What are you doing out of the truck?"

She folded her arms across her chest, and the corners of her mouth turned down. "What am I supposed to do, stay in there?"

"No. You haven't been very active, and I assumed you were tired. Of course, you can leave the truck whenever you want."

She hesitated on the doorway's threshold. "What is this place?"

Block stepped aside to let her pass. "It's an old toy factory that SoldierBots hijacked. Now we have it. Well, temporarily."

She took a few steps, eyeing the rafters and tall shelves.

"A *toy* factory. What would SoldierBots want with that?"

"Maxwell's been talking to the machines, and apparently they produce all kinds of stuff for drones and other equipment."

"Huh." Nova inspected a nearby shelf, then kicked a box. "It's all junk in here." She glanced at the panda Block held at his side.

"Do you think Wally would like this? It talks."

"Let me see." She reached for it and squeezed its middle. "It's soft." She managed a half smile and handed it back. "Yeah, I bet she'd like it."

He stuffed the panda inside his empty fire extinguisher compartment for safe keeping. It was a tight fit.

Maxwell rummaged underneath the assembly line among square storage containers. "Woop!" he shouted, making Nova flinch. "A re-matrix jump box. Freaking fantastic." He bobbed up and down on his lean, hydraulic-powered legs.

Maxwell had found the right tool, but was Vacuubot salvageable?

Chapter 9
A lot to catch up on

They banished Block from the assembly area after he'd peppered Maxwell with too many questions. Oxford assigned Block to inspect the warehouse perimeter and map out a grid two hundred yards in every direction, keeping an eye out for any discarded equipment left by SoldierBots or scavengers.

Nova went with him, perhaps not wanting to be alone with Cybel and Oxford. "So why did they kick you out again?" she asked.

"Vacuubot was my friend, and I'm hoping Maxwell can revive him."

Nova shrugged. "Seems like no big deal. Why are you so concerned? Don't you trust Maxwell to fix it?"

"It's not that. The reason Vacuubot is broken—why it consumed all but its last tiny power cells—is my fault."

"How's it your fault?"

"I abandoned Vacuubot, not realizing that was a mistake. I thought it had expired permanently."

Nova stared at the ground as they trekked through overgrown grass choked by weeds. "You didn't know. How can it be your responsibility?"

Block tried to follow her logic but couldn't see a way around it—leaving Vacuubot had definitely been his fault.

They hiked in silence until something glimmered in a patch of dry dirt. Block saw a round metal object half buried in the soil. Upon closer inspection, a broken chain enveloped it. "What is it?"

Nova unearthed it and dangled it in the air. "A locket."

Block tilted his head, not computing.

"It's a necklace you wear around your neck, and you can put things inside—pictures of people, usually." She dug at it with her thumbnail and opened it. "It's empty." She blew dirt off its surface and handed it to him.

Block inspected the dull, rose-tinted metal that definitely needed cleaning and polishing. "Whoever lost it didn't have pictures inside?"

"I guess not." Nova stuffed her hands in her pockets. "When I was a kid, my mom had a locket with a picture of me and my sister . . ." Her eyes got that faraway look that signaled distraction. "Anyway, the locket is yours now."

"Well, what do I do with it?"

"Give it away or put photos in it." She squinted. "How long are we going to be out here?"

"I'm not sure. However long it takes Maxwell to fix Vacuubot, I suppose. They'll ping me when it's time to go back." He shook the dirt from the locket's chain and tucked it inside his thigh compartment for safekeeping.

They kept working their way through knee-high weeds, following the perimeter while Block scanned it into his memory files. "What happened in Arizona?" he asked.

Nova stiffened. "What do you mean?"

"When the SoldierBots arrived."

"What's there to say? Everyone died. Story over." Her steps were heavier now.

"I'm sorry."

She grunted and kicked a rock in her way so it flew in the air and struck a tree. Block knew she must miss her friends, those who had perished. Helen had been among them.

Nova bent down and grabbed a small boulder this time and heaved it at the tree. She cried out—a slow release of something trapped inside her. To Block, it sounded like she'd been injured.

"If I'd only been there." She glared at him. "But I was a mile away, up on a hill, trying to get a signal to you."

Block backed up a step, his threat indicator flaring. Nova had been angry before, but now she seemed as raw as a wound torn open.

She balled her fists. "It was my fault. I never should've left... Maria, Heater, even that creep Fletcher... Helen." She choked on her words and squeezed her eyes shut.

Block drew closer but didn't touch her. "You didn't know they would be attacked."

"I should have known. Any officer, grunt, or soldier knows that attack is always a possibility. As their leader, I shouldn't have roamed away."

"You were only trying to help. You couldn't have known the SoldierBots would ambush them. How can it be your fault?"

But she thrust her arm out at Block as if wanting to strike. "Leave me alone." She trudged back toward the truck.

He couldn't help Nova with her pain. Her guilt at abandoning her friends reached a far deeper level than Block could process.

Block finished the perimeter job despite knowing it had been busy work. His only salvageable find had been the locket, which was useless but curious to Block, and it's not as if his assignment had kept them any safer. Oxford could fight off anyone who tried to attack, so what was the point? He backtracked to the toy factory and peeked through the doorway, lingering on the threshold. At any moment, he expected Maxwell to deliver bad news—that Vacuubot was beyond recovery.

"Come in," Oxford said from beyond the factory door. He stretched out his gigantic fist and pulled Block inside.

Block stumbled, caught himself, and neared the

assembly line. Cybel sat on the conveyor, arms crossed. Maxwell stood in front of the line, hiding whatever was on the table before him—probably a mass of mangled, lifeless parts. Unfixable.

Block walked forward slowly. "I'm sure you did everything you could."

Maxwell tilted his head, listening.

Block said, "I knew it was an impossible task. I don't even know why I asked you. If there was a chance, it was worth trying, at least I thought so."

Maxwell drummed his fingers against the line's belt. "Is he done yet?"

"Stop talking, CleanerBot," Cybel said. "You drone on endlessly. It's grating."

Block's sensors captured the suggestion as input. Having been wired to assimilate hotel guests' suggestions, he would try to tweak his language module, so he didn't talk as much. Well, nobody wanted him here, so he turned to leave, but Oxford blocked the doorway, and Nova had snuck in and stood nearby, watching.

"Go back," Oxford said. "You give up too easily."

Block spun to face Maxwell. The FactoryBot skipped aside and revealed a shiny black and green contraption resting on the assembly line. It wasn't Vacuubot—it was much larger than his friend had been. Why was Maxwell working on a different robot?

Block leaned forward and scanned the nearby bits and pieces, searching for Vacuubot's discarded remnants. At least now, he could give the machine a burial and a proper funeral.

But why had Maxwell showed him some other robot? Was this a special kind of torture?

"Have a look," Maxwell said. "Closer."

A wide, rounded top covered some kind of round metallic object. Block suspected it was a salvaged drone, but then he glimpsed the disc-shaped frame under the drone's shell. It couldn't be. He knew the body underneath. He'd carried it across a Mississippi River bridge once.

Block hesitated, and Maxwell nudged his shoulder. "Go on. You can touch it. I had to meld Vacuubot's CPU and microbial chamber with that of the toy turtle drone you see on top. Vacuubot's CPU was in terrible shape, so this was the only way I could think of to save your friend. Basically, I made it a lot stronger and better than before, and now Vacuubot can do everything a drone can do."

Block tapped a finger on the metallic armored shell that formed a dome over Vacuubot's frame. He pulled back, worried he would break it.

"Don't worry," Maxwell said. "I amped up the armored shell. It can withstand bullets and impacts of up to five-hundred pounds."

"How did you? Why?" Block's CPU swirled with so many questions, he couldn't process them fast enough to come out of his auditory unit.

"You haven't seen the best part yet." Maxwell pointed under the shell.

Block bent down to get eye level with Vacuubot's body where the core processor was located. The graphics display lit up with blue and green lights. Vacuubot's familiar digital smiley face appeared.

"Vacuubot? Is it really you?"

It's me. Hello, Block. The message came through Block's feed. His sensors buzzed, threat indicator confused, and he stumbled backward, looking frantically at Maxwell and Oxford. "Did you just get Vacuubot's message?"

Maxwell shook his head. "I programmed it to communicate with you. It's a private channel, and you don't need an open comm to talk. You're linked. That way, if you need to be cloaked, you can still communicate with Vacuubot."

Block inspected Vacuubot's display again. He messaged the machine, *Hello?*

Hello.

I'm so glad you're back! But I'm sorry I left you in Iowa. I didn't know you had an energy reserve left.

I know. It was a simple mistake. It's not your fault.

"What's happening?" Cybel asked. "Are they messaging each other?"

"I assume so," Maxwell said.

Block rose. "Vacuubot and I have a lot to catch up on."

Near the door, Oxford shifted his weight. "Let's give Block some time." He collected Cybel from her seat on the conveyor.

Maxwell hesitated. "I have a lot to explain about how Vacuubot functions now."

"Later," Oxford said as he bent his head to exit the factory.

Maxwell rested a hand on Block's shoulder. "Catch you later."

"Wait." Block tapped the top of Vacuubot's shell. "I have many questions, which we can discuss later, but I want to say thank you for fixing my friend. I don't know how to repay you."

Maxwell raised his hands. "No need to repay me. CleanerBots don't have money, anyway. It's on me, friend."

Block nodded and watched Maxwell leave. Nova lingered by the door, and Block waved. "Come over here. I want to officially introduce you to Vacuubot."

She sauntered over, shoulders hunched.

"Vacuubot, meet Nova. Nova, meet Vacuubot."

"Hey." Nova bowed slightly, but weakly, like she was embarrassed to be caught in this situation.

Hello, Nova . . . flashed on Vacuubot's screen.

She did a double take and leaned closer to inspect the body underneath the armor. "So, it's smart like you? I've never seen a drone that could communicate before." She raised her eyebrows. "Then again, I've never gotten this close to any drones before. Are you sure this is safe?"

"Of course. Vacuubot would never harm us," Block said.

"Mind if I hang here?" Nova hopped up and sat on

the assembly line. "I don't exactly feel comfortable out there with your . . . friends."

"They won't hurt you." Block walked around Vacuubot for a full view, admiring Maxwell's handiwork. "Well, I'd stay clear of Cybel, if I were you. She's the one that's a bit unpredictable."

"Why doesn't the one—what's his name, Maxwell —fix her legs?"

Block inspected Vacuubot's front. "She doesn't want to be fixed."

"Weird." Nova picked a shiny piece of scrap metal off the line and fidgeted with it.

That's mine, Vacuubot messaged Block.

"Nova, can you please put that down?"

She tossed it down as if it were a snake. "What is it?"

"I don't know, but it's part of Vacuubot."

Nova pulled her legs toward her and wrapped her arms around her knees. "What does that thing do, exactly? Does it clean like you?"

"It used to." Then Block messaged, *what other changes did Maxwell make?*

Watch, Vacuubot replied. The object Nova had grabbed rose two feet in the air. Nearby, three other mini-drones mirrored it.

Nova scooted away. "What the—?"

Vacuubot's frame buzzed and clicked as the sleek machine slowly rose and hovered. His small friend was now a drone, one that was incredibly advanced. Block glimpsed Vacuubot's full, original body underneath the midnight black and dark green armored shell, but the machine now seemed outfitted for battle.

What are you? Block messaged. *Are you still Vacuubot?*

Yes. Only much better. All the processing capabilities I had come easier than before. Vacuubot soared up to the factory's rafters and beamed aerial images of the floor layout into Block's feed.

The four drones are remnants of the Mach X drones that attacked you. To demonstrate, Vacuubot sent them veering off suddenly in all four directions, and more overhead images beamed into Block's feed.

I can process more scenarios and help you fight for Wally. The drones are weaponized, and so am I. We're ready for battle.

How do you know about Wally? Block messaged.

I listened when we were on the ride here. This private channel with you is something I asked Maxwell to do. For you.

"For me?" Block said out loud, startling Nova. *For me?*

Yes, you. I missed you, Block.

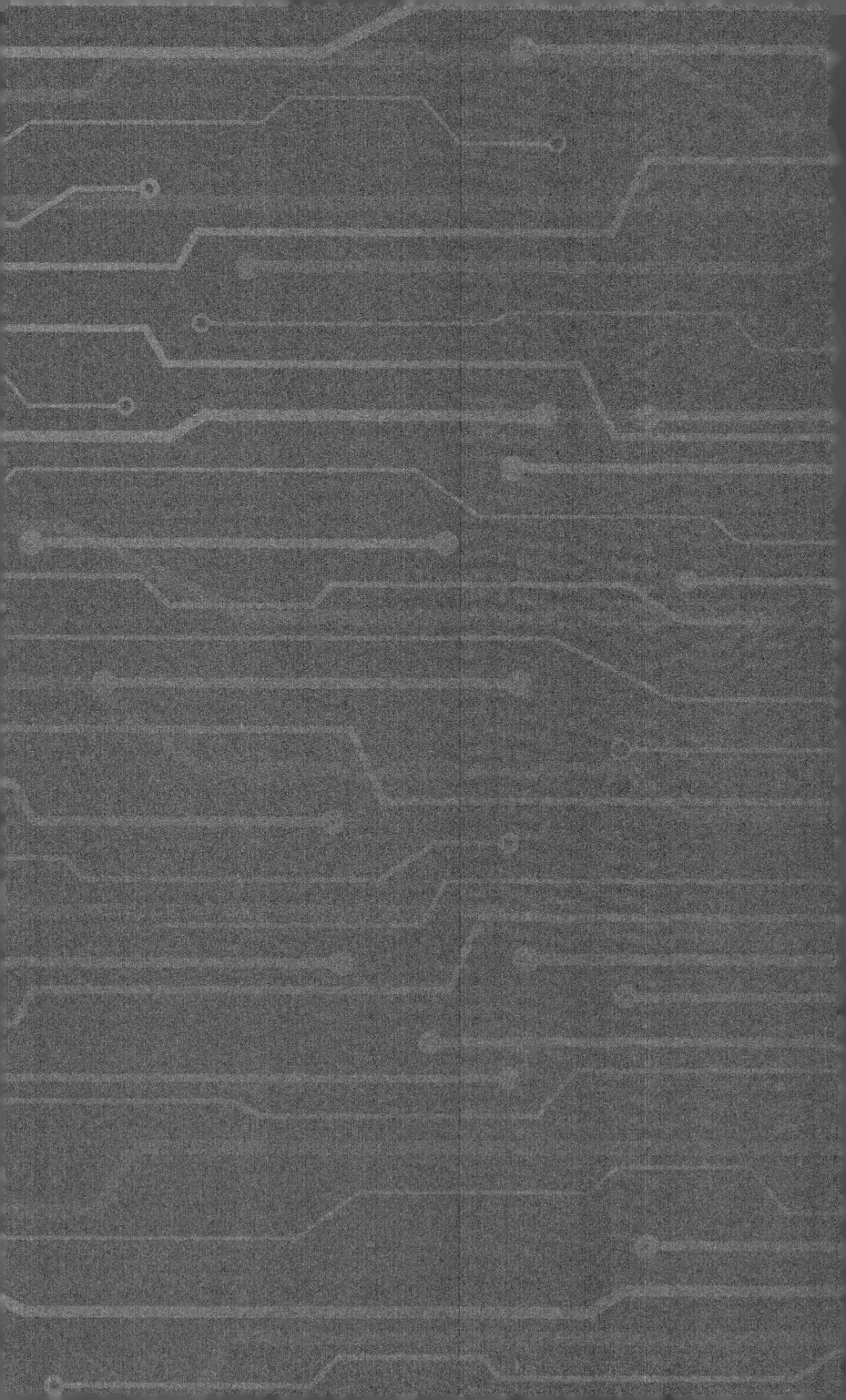

Chapter 10
Our security depends on it

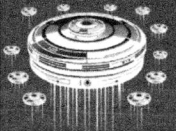

Number 21's wheels rumbled down the cracked and beaten highway as they drove east that night. Abandoned cars became more plentiful—and dangerous. Rebel survivors had set up traps, including spikes on the road meant to shred tires, but fortunately 21's sophisticated scanners could pinpoint the danger so it could stop in time. That left Maxwell, Nova, and Block to venture outside and clear away any worrisome obstacles, an event that had happened three times in the last two hours.

Inside 21's cabin, Vacuubot rested beside Block on the long bench seat. Oxford perched in his usual crushed-in spot, and Maxwell talked to Cybel in the front while Nova roamed between the bunk area and close enough to talk to Block but stayed away from Cybel's territory.

"I wish you would say something to the others," Block told her when she sat across from him.

She cast a wary glance at Oxford. "I don't trust a Mech. Not after what I've seen."

Block nodded but wished she would lighten up. He'd explained twice already that Oxford had rebelled against Mach X, but she still seemed uneasy. At least she was up and moving about, which suggested a healthy turn. He couldn't ask for too much at once.

"I just got shot," 21 remarked casually.

"What?" Maxwell bolted up from his seat on the floor.

"Don't worry. My steel is resistant. They can't hurt us."

Nova fidgeted on the bench across from Block, digging at the corners of her nail beds.

"Humans out in the wastelands," Cybel said. "Still waging their useless resistance."

"It's not useless." Nova's shoulder muscles tensed. "They're trying to survive. You didn't give us much choice."

Cybel swiveled her head toward Nova. "How is shooting at random vehicles considered surviving?"

"Cybel, that's enough," Oxford said. "Drop it."

An awkward silence hung in the air, and Block contemplated ways to change the subject. Outside the tinted windows, wild vines stretched across the asphalt and snaked through abandoned pieces of bicycles and garbage ditched on the road. Block registered all the litter and noted how much it had increased since the last time he'd traversed the highways. He had to mute himself so as not to comment on the trash and risk annoying all the others.

Nova frowned, then excused herself with a yawn. Had Cybel upset her? She hadn't woken up all that long ago, so Block assumed she must want time alone again. Retreating into the bunk area, she drew the curtain.

Block patted the top of Vacuubot's shell. "How are you doing?"

Fine. I'm excited to help you on your mission.

"I'm so glad you're back." Then Block added privately, *I'm happy we found you.*

Maxwell and Cybel talked in low voices. Maxwell swiveled his head and glanced at Block. After a minute, Maxwell waved his hand to invite him over. As Block neared, Cybel twisted her legless torso.

"What's going on?" Block asked.

"You should sit down for this." Maxwell patted the red carpet at his side. "Here is good."

Block lowered himself to 21's floor. "Is something wrong? Did I do anything wrong?"

"It's not you," Maxwell said.

Oxford leaned forward and extended his torso and neck to join in the conversation. "It's her."

"You mean, Nova?" She'd probably offended them. She was rather hopeless when it came to common courtesy.

"I'll get to the point," Cybel said. "Your human friend is lying to you."

"What? How?"

"She's spying on us, communicating with someone in secret. She's in the bunk talking to them right now."

"Talking to someone, but how?"

"She has a comm," Maxwell said. "Cybel's correct. I detected it with a scanner I snagged from the factory."

Block hadn't expected this. If Nova was communicating with someone, why wouldn't she tell him? Had he once again trusted her, only to be lied to?

He rose. "I'll talk to her."

"We need to know who she's chatting with," Cybel said.

Block halted, hesitating.

"Our security depends on it." Cybel gripped the rifle she always kept close. "If she's in touch with human rebels, she could have revealed our location. We may be intercepted. Attacked."

"She wouldn't do that," Block said.

"You don't know that," Cybel said. "She's a human, and they're loyal to each other. We're an afterthought—not on their level—or so they think."

Oxford said, "I understand she's your friend, but we need to know who she's communicating with. Cybel is right."

They all watched Block while he contemplated his strange predicament. They were angry with him, so it seemed—especially Cybel—and so he was forced to confront Nova. It was difficult being the one who had brought Nova on board in the first place. It wasn't his fault if she was doing something wrong. Or was it? This processing was beyond his comprehension. Being friends with a human was overrated.

He steeled himself for his mission. "Okay. I'll go find out." He approached the rear cabin quietly, his tread pattern tuned to the finest carpet setting, as close to tiptoeing as a robot could get. He paused when he heard Nova's soft muttering. Maybe Cybel was correct. He knocked on the cabin wall next to the bunk. Her talking stopped, and there was a thud.

"Ow." She yanked open the curtain. "Block, what is it? Why did you bang on the wall? I was sleeping."

He thrust his hands on his hips, a move she'd often made herself. "You weren't sleeping. You were talking to someone."

Her jaw dropped. "What are you talking about? Of course, I was sleep—"

"Don't lie to me. We detected your comms signal on a scanner."

She flushed two shades deeper. "All right. It's no big deal, okay? I have a comm built into my bracelet." Block recalled how she'd hidden her hand when he'd heard her talking in her sleep. She must have taken him for an idiot, so easy to fool. He'd once again fallen into the trap of trusting her.

"You lied to me again," Block said. "Who are you talking to?"

She lowered her gaze and backed against the bunk wall. "A friend."

"That's not good enough. Cybel won't hesitate to

interrogate you. She's already made Oxford suspicious."

Nova held her head high. "I won't . . . They can't." She pulled her knees to her chest atop the crumpled sheets.

Block sat on the edge of the bed. "They can, and they will make you talk if they want to. You know I'm not strong enough to fight them."

"God. Trapped in a self-driving truck with a bunch of AIs. What the hell happened in my life to deserve this?"

"Why did you come with me in the first place?"

"I didn't know what else to do after I came back . . . Everyone was dead. Helen, the others in my troop, and I couldn't find Wally. And the worst part was, I knew it was all my fault. I'd left them alone—left Wally. I knew you'd be furious."

"Me? Why would you care what I thought?"

"Because..." She stared at his faceplate and bit back her words. "It's nothing. Sometimes I forget I'm talking to an emotionless robot."

Is that how she viewed him? Technically, he didn't have emotions—couldn't possibly experience pain and suffering like humans did. And yet, he did *feel* something from time to time, especially when it came to protecting Wally and making sure his friends stayed safe.

"Who are you communicating with?" he asked.

"Before I tell you, you should know I've been

seeking answers about Wally. I'm trying to find clues about where the SoldierBots might've taken her."

"We know that already. They're taking her to Mach X in New York."

"How can you be sure?" Her eyes narrowed. "What if they want you to think she's going to New York? Lead you off track—way off track."

"Why would you say that? Do you know something about Wally's whereabouts?"

She nodded slowly. "You and your friends are looking for Wally in the wrong place."

Chapter 11
What drove her now

Block was so amped up, he could barely stop the jolt of energy reserves from flooding his hydraulics. "Tell me. What information do you have?"

Nova grabbed Block's arm and drew him onto the bed, then yanked the yellow checkered curtains shut. "I have intelligence from a very reliable source."

"Who?"

"I've been talking to Shane."

A sudden thump sounded from the narrow hallway just beyond the bunks. "I knew it! Stop this truck, right now."

Block poked his head outside the curtain. Cybel had crawled along the floor and lurked next to the wall where Nova and Block sat.

21 rolled to a jarring halt at Cybel's command, causing Block to grab onto the top edge of the upper bunk to keep from falling.

"I knew she was dangerous to have on board,"

Cybel said. "She's been on a hidden comms signal with Hemlock."

Nova raced into the aisle, chin high and fists clenched. "I contacted Shane to help Block find Wally."

Cybel wrapped a fist around her rifle. "You were giving Hemlock our location, telling them our plans. All of this is leading up to an attack. Oxford, do something."

"Let's gather outside and talk about this." Oxford looked at Cybel. "Calmly and rationally."

"What is there to be rational about? She's a spy. She just admitted it." Cybel said as Oxford hoisted her in his arms.

Block and the others climbed down 21's steps. It was 2218 hours, and a full moon glowed down on them, casting a long shadow where Oxford stood. The light cast dark pockets beneath Nova's eyes, and fatigue was etched on her face.

Maxwell hung back near 21's carbon fiber trailer skirt; Vacuubot hovered nearby, steadying itself. Flying was a novel experience for the machine, and it was quickly learning. Oxford set Cybel on the road, where she balanced herself with outspread digits. After repairing her microbial cavity, Maxwell had patched up the gaping hole where she'd been severed and filled in the empty cavities with material to support her. Despite Maxwell's offers to craft new legs or wheels for mobility, she had stubbornly refused.

"The events seem crystal clear to me," Cybel said.

"The human is communicating intelligence to Hemlock Command. Next to Mach X, Hemlock's our worst enemy."

"And what do you propose?" Oxford asked.

"We drop her. Go on our way and leave her behind."

"But there's nothing out here for miles," Block said. "We don't even know what's out here."

Nova gripped Block's arm, squeezing hard for a moment. "I can speak for myself. I don't need a CleanerBot to defend me." She stepped forward, nudging him aside. "Leave me here. I don't care. But understand this—I did not give up any information, other than to mention I was traveling with Block."

Oxford grunted. "What other evidence do you have, Cybel?"

"What other evidence do I need? She's admitted that she's been communicating with Hemlock. Allow her on the truck, and you'll bring down the human rebel forces on us."

"You've had your say." Oxford peered down at Nova. "What else do you have to answer in your defense?"

"Like I said before"—her chest puffed slightly—"I was trying to help Block by obtaining intelligence from Shane."

"Intelligence on what?" Oxford asked.

"When were you going to tell us?" Cybel asked.

"I ask the questions!" Oxford struck his fist against

the road, causing a minor tremor. Even Nova, with her stubborn bravado, backed up a step.

"What intelligence?" Oxford repeated.

Unsure of what machine programming propelled him, Block stepped forward. "Shane was Nova's boyfriend. He's in charge of Hemlock and—"

"No." Nova's glare reflected the silver moon. "Let me answer the questions. Stay out of this."

Block retreated; his timidity module vibrated when yelled at.

"I said nothing because I didn't want to risk your suspicion, which is exactly what's happening now." Nova straightened her spine and planted her feet firmly. "You're all jumping to the conclusion that I'm planning an attack on you. It's totally ridiculous."

Oxford and Cybel exchanged a glance. "Go on," Oxford said to Nova.

"Yes, Shane and I were once a couple, but no more." She crossed her arms. "We'e still civil, and in parting, we agreed to go our separate ways. Shane never trusted Block and didn't understand our ... relationship."

"Is this true?" Oxford asked, and Block nodded. There was so much more Block could have added about how poorly the human rebel troops had treated him, how they'd kept him apart from Wally, how much they'd abhorred robots. But what was the point now? Nova had misled him repeatedly, first making him come to New Denver, supposedly a peaceful place, when it was actually a war zone against his kind. Then she'd taken Wally from him—the worst betrayal of all.

He could never believe she was truthful ever again; of that he was certain. But Nova always had a motive—there was invariably something in it for her—and he wondered what drove her now.

"Shane gave me a communicator, said that if I ran into trouble to let him know, and he would help if he could." Nova shrugged. "I told him it wasn't necessary, but he insisted."

"I'm not buying it," Cybel said.

"Let her finish." Oxford stomped against the pavement, and Maxwell ducked beneath the truck.

I believe her, Vacuubot messaged Block privately. But what did such a small, primitive machine know about people?

Nova said, "When X's forces killed my group in Arizona, I was devastated. You don't know what that's like . . . the survivor guilt—"

"I know it," Oxford said. "Cybel understands it too."

"Right. I forgot you lost your soldiers." Nova hung her head for a moment before she went on. "I had no choice but to come with you. I was despondent, and Block helped me. I was nervous to be around all of you, so I reached out to Shane. But I didn't give him any details, I swear. I said we're on the move." She paused, checking for a reaction. "Shane's been tracking X's forces as they move east. I told him what happened to my people—how they all died. He was understandably angry and sad and furious. Many of them, he was close to. He trained them."

Maxwell clutched his hands together. "I regret not saying it before. I'm sorry for your loss."

"Me too," Block said.

"As am I," Oxford said. "I know what it's like to lose your followers. Your friends."

Nova shivered, though the night was mild. "Thanks."

"Then what happened? What else did you tell Hemlock?" Cybel asked.

"Give her a moment," Oxford said.

"It's fine." Nova crossed her arms. "Shane and his army have tracked X's troops to a compound in Chicago."

Chicago. Block's circuitry buzzed with approval.

"He believes it's the same cluster that killed my people and abducted Wally. Hemlock has been tracking them, staking them out, and is planning an attack. Shane's forces are hunkered down in the west side of the city."

Block rushed forward, his programming propelling him as if a hotel guest needed help. "They took Wally to Chicago?"

"That's what Shane told me."

"And you believe him?"

Nova nodded and bit her lip.

Wally was in Chicago—in Block's home city! He raced toward Oxford and Cybel, waving his arms.

"We must leave for Chicago. Right now."

Chapter 12
Bigger than his original design

The Chicago skyline loomed in the distance, eerie and spectral, as a gray fog enveloped the buildings. From fifteen miles away, the skyscraper tops seemed to float in clouds.

"Exactly how are you planning to infiltrate the old Sears tower?" Cybel asked. She'd been listening in silence as Nova described where Mach X's troops had allegedly taken Wally.

Nova shook her head. "I don't know. That's why we need Shane's help. They're the ones who have been studying the SoldierBot movements. They're the ones planning the attack."

"And once you arrive?" Cybel asked. "You're going to stroll up and say, 'Hey it's me, Nova. By the way, here's a war Mech that used to be one of Mach X's generals?' I'm sure Shane will greet you with open arms."

Nova turned and paced a circle in the roadside

gravel. Dawn was lifting the darkness from the edges of the sky. On the stretch of highway where they'd stopped after hours of driving, a commercial van lay on its side with glass shattered all around it. Curious, Maxwell explored it for parts and climbed on top of the vehicle to see what was painted on its side. "Tortillas!" he said. "This van was once used to deliver tortillas from a factory."

"Bravo, Sherlock Holmes," Cybel said. "Now shut up."

"I found some fluids we can use," Maxwell added, ignoring Cybel.

Nova continued, "It's a guarantee that Shane and his people will feel threatened." She stared up at the Mech. "Oxford is pretty damn scary."

He nodded. "Tell them I mean no harm, that I'm working with you."

"Don't be ridiculous, Oxford," Cybel said. "You know how the humans are. Shoot first and ask questions later. If they got you in the CPU—"

"Maxwell could fix him, right?" Block asked.

"Nope." Maxwell popped out from behind the van. "A direct hit in the CPU—that's unfixable."

"I could communicate with Shane," Nova said. "Tell him what to expect and to tell his people to stand down."

But Cybel shook her head. "No. We can't risk what would happen if even one of his soldiers ignored his orders, or if there was a communication gap." She scooted several inches on the pavement using her long arms. "Do you want to be responsible for bringing down Oxford? He's our only hope of taking out Mach X."

Nova clenched her teeth, and Block knew she was going to say something in anger or do something rash. He wanted to say something to help, but he wasn't sure what would.

"I'll go on my own," Nova said. "That way, nobody has to risk themselves. I'll meet with Shane and convince him to let me join their attack. I'll search for Wally and"—she turned to Block— "bring her to you if I find her."

But Block's logic processor churned. In the past, Nova had lied and kept Wally away from him, had kept her with humans.

"That's a wise choice," Cybel said. "That way, Oxford and I are not at risk."

"Fine. Then that's the way it'll be." Nova strode down the highway past the van.

"Where's she going?" Maxwell asked.

"I think she wants to be alone," Block said. Who could blame her? Cybel was anything but friendly.

"She's going to alert Shane that she's coming," Cybel said. "And likely she's telling them about me and Oxford. Giving away our position."

"Enough," Oxford said, and stomped away in the opposite direction.

Maxwell trotted over, carrying a rusty piece of metal and an old hybrid car battery. "Guess Oxford wants to be alone too?"

A buzz sounded, and Vacuubot soared into view. The drone had surveyed the area to make sure there were no threats nearby. Images from its camera flooded Block's feed, and he straightened, jerking his arms when he viewed the footage.

"What is it?" Cybel asked.

Block processed. "Vacuubot, you went very far. I didn't know you could—"

"Is there danger approaching?" Cybel balled her fists against the pavement. "Stop blabbering and get to the point."

"Well, we can't continue along the highway," Block said. "The SoldierBots have set up checkpoints into the city. We're only 2.5 miles from one."

"I suspected as much," Cybel said. "Are you all cloaked?"

Block nodded and Maxwell confirmed.

"Nova can set off on her own and figure out how to get past the checkpoint."

"What? That would be dangerous," Block said. "We can't expect her to survive a SoldierBot checkpoint. We have to help her somehow."

"And risk a battle? I don't think so," Cybel said. "They may be patrolling and could've spotted us already."

"My sky camouflage is enabled," 21 said. "Any patrolling drones won't pick me up."

"See," Block said. "We can help Nova. According to Vacuubot's footage, there are five SoldierBots at the guard station. Oxford could easily take care of them."

"And risk getting damaged just to get the human into the city? Not a wise scenario."

"There has to be something we can do." Block looked at Maxwell who shrugged.

"I have an idea," 21 said.

Ten minutes later, Block approached Nova where she sat on the hood of an old blue Prius. Something had crushed its roof, as if a Mech had walked by and slammed a fist on top of the car.

"How are you doing?" he asked.

"Hey." She slid over, giving him room to hop up on the car.

Vacuubot hovered, watching but giving them distance. Was the machine being protective? Or curious?

"So, you told Shane that you're coming?"

She nodded and rested her elbows on her raised knees. "Yeah, he's expecting me."

"Where is he?"

"Twin towers on the river. He said they look like honeycombs, and that I can't miss them. Do you know it?"

"Yes. I know of those towers, although I've never been there."

She sighed. "He and his troops have taken the towers over. They had to clear out some salvaging bots, but otherwise the SoldierBots have ignored it for whatever reason. Damaged from flooding and left to rot, it sounds like."

Block processed scenarios, but there was a missing piece of his calculations. "Why would Shane help you?"

"I told him I had intelligence from Oxford being a general, that he gave me some secrets, but I'll only tell Shane in person." She paused and glanced at Block, then nudged her shoulder against his. "I said I would give up the intelligence in exchange for getting Wally out."

She said, 'getting Wally out,' not getting Wally out *and* handing her to Block. That meant Shane could keep her, and that was a scenario Block could not abide. Shane knew how important Wally was to Mach X.

Rather than confront Nova on this point, he asked, "How can you trust Shane?"

"He's a man of his word—at least, he was when I knew him well. I suppose he could lie and not help me get Wally out, but I don't see why he would." She shifted to face him. "Why do you ask? What's bothering you?"

He wasn't certain he could trust her. But instead, he said, "I'll go with you."

"What?" She flashed a startled grin. "You're not serious." She hopped off the car's hood. "You want to come with me and face Shane and all his troops again?"

"You can't do this on your own." His real motivation was to be closer to Wally, but if he confessed that, she might shut him down.

"And why not?"

"For one thing, you're going to need help getting past the checkpoint that's 2.5 miles down the road. And I have a plan for that thanks to 21."

She jerked her head in that direction and narrowed her eyes. "Fine. I'm listening. What else?"

"I have a surveillance tool." He pointed up at Vacuubot, who hovered nearby. "Vacuubot can get places that Shane's spies can't."

"Shane said he has drones, that his people built non-sentient ones."

"SoldierBots can pick those off like sitting ducks. If they haven't yet, X's troops are probably feeding them false intel. Even a CleanerBot knows that much."

Nova shook her head. "Crap. Is that really true?"

"Ask Oxford or Cybel."

She balled her fists behind her neck, looked skyward, and cursed. "If I take you, you won't slow me down?"

"Not at all," Block said, sliding off the car. "In fact, I'll get you there faster and in one piece. Once we get past the checkpoint, Vacuubot has staked out a location where the others can hunker down and wait for us."

"You've really thought this through, haven't you?"

"I've processed a lot of scenarios. We can do this. We *have* to do this." For the first time ever, Block felt bigger than his original design.

He had a plan.

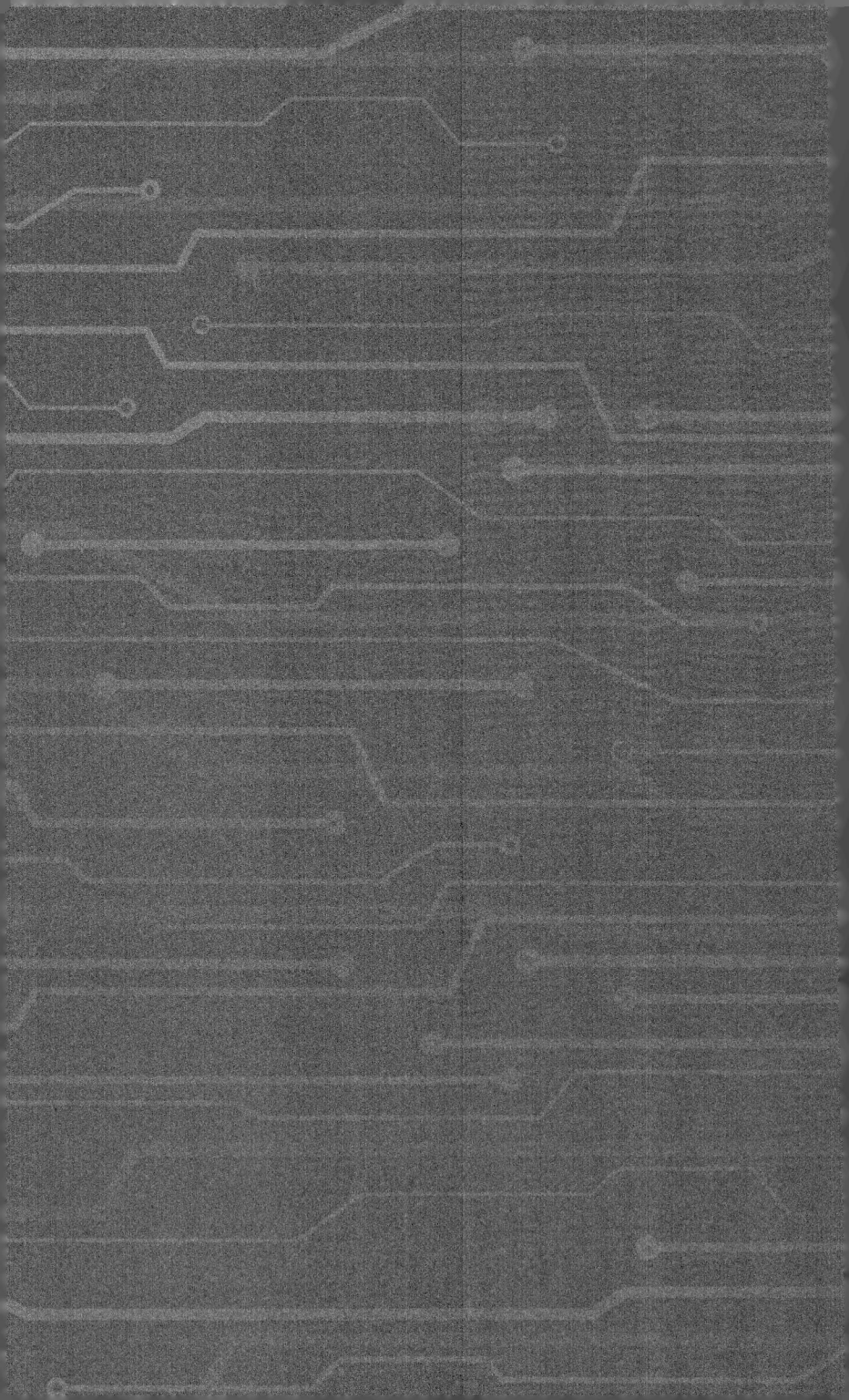

Chapter 13
Splunk. Kerplooey!

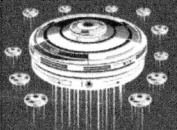

"I hope this works," Block said. "Nova, keep your head down."

"This is humiliating," Cybel said. She sat on 21's floor in the aisle way, sandwiched between Block and Nova and handcuffed to both. A bed sheet had been draped over all of them.

Oxford, we're here, Block messaged inaudibly as they approached the highway checkpoint that led into Chicago.

I'm ready, he replied.

But Block's threat indicator buzzed. Vacuubot's preliminary scan had been wrong. *We're at the checkpoint, but there's a problem.*

Cybel picked it up by eavesdropping. "What's wrong?"

"Eight SoldierBots, not five," Block said. "There's no way we can make it."

"Stick with the plan," Cybel said. Then she

messaged them privately, *Oxford will take care of the SoldierBots if it comes down to it.*

If we can't get past, I'll take out as many as I can, Oxford confirmed.

A SoldierBot approached the window; its black armor glistened in the sun, and dark scopes covered its optics. A security drone circled 21's side and headed to the rear of the semi.

"Howdy," Maxwell said from the driver seat. He was trying to pass himself off as a serious truck driving courier, but he couldn't help being a goof. He wore a human's cap with the emblem of a team called the Chicago Bears that he'd scavenged from a car. "How can I help you?"

"Are you carrying anything flammable?" the SoldierBot asked.

"No, sir." Maxwell's voice was deep, cheery, and human sounding.

"Let me scan your orders."

Cybel had warned them about the cube-shaped transmitter that any robots carrying on business under Mach X's authority were required to present at all times, including couriers.

"The thing is . . ." Maxwell drummed his metal fingers on 21's cockpit. "My cube got wet and went splunk. Kerplooey!"

"What? You destroyed the cube containing your orders?"

A second SoldierBot joined the interrogator. "What's the problem?"

"It was an accident," Maxwell said. "I dropped it in a huge puddle of blood when I was killing a couple of angry humans 136.2 miles ago. It fizzed out."

The first SoldierBot turned to the other. "This one lost his cube. No orders."

"You can't proceed any further without orders." The second SoldierBot was the superior, as Block had guessed.

"I understand," Maxwell said. "Rules are rules."

"I'll permit you to turn around and travel back where you came from," the SoldierBot supervisor said.

Maxwell tipped his cap. "Say, can you direct me where I might go to retrieve a new cube with my orders? This stuff I'm carrying has an expiration date."

"You'll have to go back to where you got your orders."

"All the way to Tulsa? Oh, drat!" Maxwell was laying it on thick. Block was sure he was going to get a stern lecture from Cybel and Oxford later on.

What are you carrying?" the Supervisor asked.

"Cough syrup, glue, a hundred ballpoint pens, a vacuum cleaner drone, and a bottle of gin." The inventory was real—all of the items, minus Vacuubot, had been discovered inside 21's drawers and cabinets. They were banking on the SoldierBots not getting too curious.

"Passengers?"

"Yes, I'm transporting passengers. There's a useless CleanerBot model—X4J6—it calls itself. A TrackerBot torso—no legs. Rather sad, actually. And a human.

Found her half-starving and thought someone might have some use for her."

A third SoldierBot jogged to the window. "We have conducted a preliminary scan of the cargo. It's clean. However—"

"That's a relief," Maxwell said. "I much prefer being clean—"

"Do you ever shut up?" asked the supervisor. "Go on," he told the other.

"There's something strange on the truck."

Block's sensors flared. Nova's heart rate soared, and Cybel sat as still as granite. "They figured it out," he whispered.

"Quiet," Cybel said.

Maxwell waited. Block couldn't ping him or else the SoldierBots would pick up the transmission. The only one Maxwell could talk to was Number 21.

"This truck is hauling a smaller truck behind it," the most junior SoldierBot said.

"Driver, you did not declare an additional truck," the supervisor shouted.

"Sorry. I was getting to that."

"Explain."

"You see the sign on the truck? Trudy's Tasty Tortillas. You don't come across that every day," Maxwell said. "You know what tortillas are?"

"I know a tortilla is a food for humans," the supervisor said.

The junior SoldierBot chimed in. "I don't mean to

slow you down, sir, but I'm curious as to what this driver is up to."

"Do you question me?" the supervisor shot back. "Go to the next waiting vehicle. Out of my sight."

The dismissed SoldierBot wasted no time in getting away.

"What are you chattering on about, Driver?"

"Tortillas are a fried food—quite tasty from what I heard when I worked the Factories before the Uprising. Thanks be to Mach X!"

The Supervisor stomped a boot. "I have little knowledge of human food. This is a waste of my time. What is your point?"

"Hold on," Maxwell said. "Do you know how tortillas are made?"

No answer from the Bot.

"I was just about to tell you. Tortillas are fried in grease. There's a whole vat of the stuff in that truck, and you can have it."

There was a long pause.

"Ta-da!" Maxwell said. "It's fuel for you and your soldiers. See, I knew you were going to be cross about me losing my cube, and I hauled this truck full of fryer grease all this way to offer up as a peacemaker. If you let me pass through, I promise I'll get my shipment delivered and head back to Tulsa as soon as I can to get a new cube."

"Driver," the supervisor said softly, menacingly. "If I find you are lying, I will have you delivered to a cube-farm to be chopped up."

"My oath, sir . . . SoldierBot! You surely will be pleased with this fryer grease that I hauled for you."

There was a break as the SoldierBots must have stepped away from the window to confer and check on the truck. After another minute, the original SoldierBot returned.

"Driver, you are cleared to pass. You are to proceed immediately to your destination, talk to no one, and never return through this checkpoint again. Do you understand?"

"Thank you, kindly," Maxwell said. "Understood."

21 powered up its engine and accelerated past the guards.

Nova sighed in relief as she kicked the sheet off her head. "They didn't even come check on us."

"Not so fast," Cybel said. "We need to get clear of those jerks. They could change their mind and chase us down. We need to be sure."

"See, I can handle a border check," Maxwell said. "Nothing to it. Not a problem."

"You nearly got us destroyed, idiot," Cybel said.

"When he said cube farm, my core nearly frizzed out." Maxwell said. "I knew we had Oxford for backup."

They drove far enough past the checkpoint to where Maxwell could no longer see the SoldierBot station in the rear camera.

"Oxford, you okay up there?" Block asked.

A giant leg extended down the windshield. 21's

frame shifted from side to side as Oxford climbed off the roof.

"Watch the paint job!" 21 said.

Oxford hurried inside the cabin, bending his head and taking his usual spot. "That was excruciating."

"I can't believe they didn't see you riding on top," Block said.

"I can," Cybel said. "The SoldierBots are brainless, short-sighted wirejobs."

They had just rounded a corner when they saw a cloud of dust, heading straight for them. Two motorbikes sped toward them.

"Cloak your comms, all of you," Oxford said.

Block pulled the sheet over his head, but Nova ignored him. "Put it on," he told her.

She rolled her eyes and tossed it away. "I'm not wearing that again."

"Finally, we agree on something," Cybel said.

"SoldierBots," 21 said. "And they're in pursuit, ordering me to pull over."

"Can you evade them?" Oxford asked.

"Can I? I told you I'm a special edition with an advanced turbocharger."

"Take that exit." Nova pointed to a raised ramp that led off the highway onto a city avenue. "Quick! Before you miss it."

21 ignored her. "I don't follow orders from humans."

The biker SoldierBots took the exit, accelerated up

the frontage road, across the turnoff, and cut across in front of the semi.

The semi came to a sudden halt, and the SoldierBots opened fire with machine guns.

"Get us out of here!" Nova said as she braced herself against Block's back.

"Ready yourselves. Something's happening," Maxwell said as a myriad of purple and yellow lights flooded 21's dashboard.

"I'm about to engage thrusters," 21 said.

Block caught a glimpse of what looked like atomic torches at the rear of the cabin.

"Do it!" Oxford yelled as drones rained fire down on the roof.

The semi lurched forward as 21's thrusters fired.

The thrusters had enough force to rocket them forward, blast past the SoldierBots, and clear two miles in forty seconds.

"Nice driving," Block said as the SoldierBots became distant specks.

Chapter 14
Show yourself

"This is quite the hideout." Oxford pointed at a flock of Canadian geese that had taken over Runway Two at the abandoned O'Hare airport.

Nova descended the ladder from 21's roof and hopped the last step before joining Block. "Why would the SoldierBots leave the airport be? You'd think they'd want to command from here."

Cybel, resting on a gate area waiting chair that they'd scrounged, said, "Air travel was strategic for humans, but once Mach X crashed the markets and people were ordered to stay home, the need for air travel practically vanished overnight."

Oxford nodded. "Mach X prefers helicopters and sentient jets. A lot of new tech that had been under military development was classified. X has it all now."

While Nova ventured inside the terminal to find running water and food, Oxford reached onto 21's roof and pulled down a long rectangular box. Maxwell nodded at him as he carried it forward.

"What's in there?" Block asked.

"A surprise for Cybel." Oxford set the long box in front of her.

"What's in it?" she asked.

"Open and see."

There wasn't an easy way for her to get off her chair gracefully. She raised her chin. "This is ridic—"

"I can help," Block offered.

"Fine." She looked away.

Block unlatched the sides of the steel box. Two midnight-black steel legs rested inside. They were the powerful legs of an advanced SoldierBot.

"They're thinner and way stronger than your other legs," Maxwell said.

Oxford nodded. "You deserve the best."

Cybel stared and her silence seemed to overshadow the airport's runways.

Oxford and Maxwell glanced at each other, waiting and likely exchanging worried pings.

"You two did this," she said, finally.

"Yes," Oxford said. "We found the tools in the abandoned toy factory. I arranged for Kip to bring me the spare parts."

"You wasted your time. I don't need legs."

"Cybel, listen," Oxford said. "How many times have I told you to give up your stubborn attitude?"

She tilted her head for an instant. "38.5 times exactly. The half was when I cut you off."

"We're in danger. We won't necessarily have Number 21 to drive us. What happens when SoldierBots or humans attack?"

"I have my rifle."

Block stepped forward and ran his polisher along the thigh of one of the replacement legs. "This is the finest steel I've ever laid a brush on."

"Spare me," Cybel said.

Block sifted through his pre-programmed negotiation module for what to do. Flattery didn't work on Cybel, and neither had Oxford's attempts at reason. Block needed a new tactic, so he beamed her an image from his archive.

She jerked her head. "What's this?"

"That is Wally shortly after I found her."

"So? I'm aware of the child."

In the snapshot image, Wally was small and wrapped in a blanket. Her tiny mouth puckered with hunger and distress. "She was just a helpless human baby when I found her." Block sorted his memory files and chose another image but held it back.

Cybel drummed her fingers on the chair's armrest as she studied the sophisticated limbs. The polished black chrome gleamed in the sunlight.

"You and a horde of SoldierBots tracked her. I was the only one who looked out for her. She's an orphan."

"Why are you telling me things I already know?"

"Because we're the only ones who can help her. Mach X could be hurting her. No one else is looking out for her."

"That's not my problem."

"I know that," Block said. "But I'm hoping Oxford, Maxwell, 21, and *you* will help me find her and get her away from X."

Silence.

He beamed her the video he'd found.

"What is—"

Block waited a few seconds. "It's from when we were in the desert mine. Wally learned to recognize you. Her eyes lit up when you entered the room. She liked your face plate, I think."

"What is *Sasa*? Why is she saying that?"

"She was trying to say your name."

Cybel sat for a long moment, processing. "I said I don't need legs."

"I give up," Oxford said. He started walking away, followed by Maxwell.

Block turned and headed after them.

"But I need *these* legs," Cybel called out.

Block summoned Vacuubot, messaging the machine privately. *We're about ready to leave.*

The powerful cleaner drone zoomed over and landed nearby on the tarmac. "What will you do while we're gone?" Block asked the group.

"Well, I have a lot to do," Maxwell said. He carried an armful of tools and metal scraps he'd already scavenged in the few hours since they'd arrived.

"We'll guard Number 21 and look for fuel sources." Oxford scanned the runways and the perimeter, which was nothing but an overgrown field run by geese at the moment. "Guard against any intruders." Warm morning sunbeams cast a soft glow against his scratched, bulletproof armor.

"Well"—Nova hoisted a backpack stuffed with water, food, and tools—"This is sweet. Really, it's like a robot family postcard, but we should get moving, Block. It's going to be dark in the tunnels."

Block reached out his hand, and Oxford seized it gently. "Good luck," Oxford said.

"I wish we could keep an open channel," Maxwell said.

Cybel shifted back and forth, testing her new armored legs. "Too dangerous."

Block glanced at her as he held out his fist for Maxwell to shake. "I don't want to put you in danger. It's risky enough for me and Nova to head into the city. If they found out you were here . . ." Mach X discovering his renegade general could not be a good idea.

Maxwell took his fist, but instead of shaking it, he wrapped his metal hands around Block's. "Be safe and well, my friend. Try not to get so hurt that I can't fix you." Maxwell pointed at Nova. "That goes for you too."

She scoffed and glanced away.

Block approached Cybel, still unaccustomed to

looking up at her again. "Goodbye, Cybel. I hope to see you again soon."

She nodded once. It was all he could expect.

Nova and Block walked along the tarmac, and he looked back eventually, but Oxford and the outline of 21 had faded into a speck.

"Do you think they'll be okay there?" Block asked.

"With Oxford? Of course, he's a monster. They'll be fine." She sighed. "As long as no SoldierBots come out here."

They had to walk along exit roads and ramps that led out of the airport and onto what was once a busy expressway. A sign said *Downtown Loop* and pointed right.

"You said there were tracks, right? Where are they?" Nova asked.

"I thought we'd see them right away." Block halted and scanned the area for any sign of the abandoned train tracks that Vacuubot had told him about when an image flashed into his feed, sent by one of Vacuubot's drones.

"Where are you?" Block's circuitry buzzed, and he spun, searching the sky.

"What is it?" Nova's eyes grew wide, and she clutched the SoldierBot rifle that she'd taken.

"They're here somewhere."

"They?" Nova gritted her teeth and aimed the rifle, searching for threats.

"They, meaning Vacuubot. Come out," he said. *Show yourself,* he messaged.

Nothing.

"What are you going on about?" Nova scratched her head. "Are you okay? Are you glitching?"

Block ignored her and tilted his head. "We go no further until Vacuubot shows itself."

After several seconds, there was a faint rustling and the whir of a motor as Vacuubot appeared from behind an abandoned car and approached slowly, flying low. The four drones were tucked into side compartments.

"Hey, little guy," Nova said.

Block folded his arms and stomped his foot. "It's not a guy, and we're not happy to see it."

"We aren't?" Nova shrugged.

"Absolutely not. I ordered Vacuubot to stay behind with the others, and it defied my orders."

The machine buzzed, whirred, flashed a sad face, then settled on the pavement.

"Geez. I don't know what kind of weird robot relationships you have going on, but we have to get going. It's going to take us hours to walk into the city. We don't know what we could encounter along the tracks and in the tunnels." Nova pointed at Vacuubot. "If that thing can help us—fly around and alert us to danger nearby—then for crying out loud, let it come with."

If Block had had an annoyance indicator, it would've been registering at full strength. *You defied my orders*, Block messaged Vacuubot.

I am sorry, but Nova is right. I can help you.

Block shook his head. *I have to do this on my own.*

But you're not. Nova is with you, and it looks like you two could use all the help you can get.

Vacuubot had a good point, but something in Block wanted to prove that he was capable, that he was more than just a CleanerBot.

Nova shouldered her rifle. "Let's go. Make a decision. Flip a coin. Do whatever you have to do."

"Leave it to chance?" Block had never made decisions randomly. That went against all logic.

"Ugh." Nova dug in her pockets and retrieved a quarter. "Haven't you ever flipped a coin? Heads or tails, Block?"

"Heads or tails, what?"

"Just pick one!" Nova said.

"Tails."

She tossed the coin high in the air, caught it, and slapped it hard on one hand. "Heads." She spun and strode away.

"What does that mean?" Block asked.

It means I come with you, Vacuubot said.

They walked the dilapidated El tracks. Station signs had been graffitied over, but the few that remained identified the route as the Blue Line from the airport into the city. On either side of the raised platform were the lanes of the Expressway. The closer they got to the city, the more cars that sat abandoned, rusting and exposed to the elements.

Nova studied the cars as they walked.

"You're not thinking about going down there and searching those cars, are you?" Block asked.

"No. Those cars were scavenged and cleaned out ages ago."

"They were? How can you tell?"

"See that?" She pointed at a city bus that now occupied half of the road. All of the windows had been smashed and a circle inside a sideways triangle had been spray-painted across the side. "The sideways triangle . . . It's code for stand strong, go forward. It's meant to say that human resistors are in the area, to signal others."

"There are humans here?" Block glanced behind him and made sure Vacuubot followed. *Don't wander far*, he messaged. Vacuubot trailed behind at shoulder height.

"There might've been humans here . . . once. It's hard to say." Apartment style buildings lined the highway, long neglected. Plywood boards covered up the windows, and pitch-black scorch marks stretched across some. "We should keep moving."

"I won't argue." Block quickened his pace to match Nova's step. He'd never been through this part of the city before, had never had reason to leave the hotel, and he'd taken a different route West when he'd departed the city after the Uprising.

"How will Shane react once we arrive?" Block asked.

Nova shrugged. "He's expecting me, but he's going to take some convincing."

"Is he expecting me?"

She flinched ever so slightly, enough that Block recognized it with his enhanced motion detector. "Not exactly. I didn't mention that you're coming."

Block halted. "Why not?"

She rolled her eyes. "Why are you stopping? We need to keep going." She glanced nervously at the wall that separated the highway from the housing beyond.

"You didn't answer my question. Why didn't you tell Shane that I'm coming?"

"Because I didn't want an argument about it. I thought it would be better to show up and just have you with me. Also, I didn't want them thinking about it and deciding something in the time it takes us to get there. Got it?"

Block turned to say more when suddenly the track below him seemed to vomit up rocks.

"Run!" Nova shouted. She bolted toward the next station, two hundred yards away.

Block stumbled at first, then sprinted after her, checking over his shoulder, but Vacuubot flew at his side, and the little machine flipped sideways so that its armored turtle shell faced the direction of the gunfire. Block's metal boots thudded against the dirty concrete. Ahead, Nova had reached the shelter of two large cement columns in the station. Her back pressed against the wall, and she waved at Block to hurry.

With each crack of the sniper's rifle, Vacuubot took the hit. Its armor deflected the shots, but the impact hammered the drone off course. Vacuubot struggled to stay upright and in the air.

Something snagged Block's foot—a tie or large rock. The ground flew up as he fell, and he landed on his elbows and tried to push the ground away with his hands. The shooting ceased for a moment, and Vacuubot circled back, hovering over Block. Then Vacuubot rose up and launched two drones from its undercarriage. They soared high in the air and headed toward the area where the shooting must have been coming from—a patch of trees that had somehow thrived on this barren stretch of highway. The drones strafed the area with bullets.

Get up, Vacuubot said. *My drones will occupy the shooters.*

Block slowly got on his knees and then stood, clearing the distance to the next station awkwardly. He reached Nova and collapsed on the hard cement.

Chapter 15
Served its purpose

Nova slid down the wall, clutching her rifle, and seized Block's shoulder. "Are you all right?"

"Checking for damage," he said. Vacuubot landed at his feet.

"I saw what your drone did," she said. "It protected you."

Block's processor churned as it assessed the damage to his legs and feet from concrete shrapnel and the impact from his fall. Vacuubot's shell had a dent the size of a dinner plate extending halfway across its back. The metal edge near its bottom left side had been shredded.

Are you damaged? Block messaged.

It's not bad.

It occurred to Block that he would be lying dead on the tracks right now had Vacuubot not been there. He tapped the small machine's back as if acknowledging it.

You're welcome.

Nova stood and gripped her rifle, then peered around the column. The assault from Vacuubot's drones had silenced the attackers.

"What's going on out there?" Block asked.

"Your friend's drones scared the shooters away."

"Who were they? SoldierBots?"

"Probably randoms who saw a shiny robot walking along the track and thought you'd make good target practice." She fished a tin of water out of her pack and chugged it.

"But they could have shot you too."

"They might not care. I'm a human walking alongside a robot and a drone. They probably thought they were doing me a favor, that you'd captured me."

Her logic made sense. There were few reasons that humans and robots would travel together, and usually it was for bad reasons.

Block's damage report appeared in his feed—the toe of his right boot had been cracked, and already repair nanobots had been dispatched to try and fix it enough for him to keep walking. He stared at his palms. A few scratches marred the chrome surface, but he could buff those out later. He'd been lucky. "What now?"

"What does your friend say?" Nova asked. "Flying turtle is the one with the drones. Are the shooters gone?"

I'm calling the drones back, Vacuubot messaged. Within seconds, one of the drones landed next to Vacuubot who lifted up its side and absorbed the drone beneath its shell.

"Where's the other one?" Block asked.

He was answered by a high-pitched whining buzz. The second drone skidded across the track and bounced, black smoke pouring out of its center, until it crashed against a concrete barrier.

"I guess that answers your question." Nova wasn't trying to be a wise ass, at least Block didn't think so.

It's okay, Vacuubot said. *The drone served its purpose.*

"Do you want to try to fix it? You don't plan to leave it, do you?" Block asked.

Leave it.

"Is the sniper gone?" Nova asked.

"Vacuubot says it's clear."

She tossed the tin water can down on the ground. Block paused and glanced at the refuse, a question nearly out of his voice box.

"Oh, come on. You're not serious. You're going to lecture me about littering at a time like this?"

Block watched her in silence.

She clenched her jaw, shook her head, and picked up the can, stuffing it in her pack. "I can't believe you."

They jogged the tracks now. Block couldn't run at full speed owing to his injury, but the nanobots had done their job, and he was able to keep up with Nova. Every so often, he glanced at Vacuubot, grateful to have the hybrid cleaner drone on their mission.

He caught Nova studying Vacuubot a few times

when she thought Block wouldn't notice. After an hour of jogging, she was out of breath, and sweat poured down her cheeks. They'd reached a place where the high walls surrounding the track obscured them from view of the highway and outskirts.

"Let's take a break." She threw off her pack and balanced her rifle next to it, not far from reach, then cracked the lid of another water can and drank it in four gulps.

Block leaned against the wall across from her, and Vacuubot settled beside him. He reached into his thigh storage compartment and pulled out a plastic pouch that contained a dark brown liquid. His metal blade sliced into it, and he offered some to Vacuubot first. A small metal tube extended from Vacuubot's side to suck in part of the liquid. When it was done, Block connected his feeding tube and finished the bag.

Nova wiped her mouth with the back of her hand. "What is that stuff?"

"Fuel cocktail. Maxwell put these together. Old jet fuel from some of the planes."

"Tasty." Nova bit into a protein bar, chewing loudly.

"Vacuubot says we're approaching the part where the train goes underground. We both have night vision—"

"I'll be fine." Nova pulled out a circular band, wrapped it around her head, and adjusted until a flashlight rested on her forehead. "Maxwell made something for me too." She smirked.

"Good idea," Block said. "What do you think we'll find in those tunnels?"

She leaned back, narrowed her eyes. "Could be more humans. Scavengers. Or we could be going into a rebel hotspot."

"Oh, no."

"But I doubt it. If there was a human rebel hideout, the SoldierBots would've cleaned it out. I think we'll find stragglers." She looked at Block, all traces of humor gone. "Listen carefully. If we run into humans, let me do the talking. I'll say that I own you, that you serve me. Both of you."

"I see," Block said. "I'll have to explain this concept to Vacuubot."

Don't bother. I'm not dumb.

"It's for your own good," Nova said. "As we saw with our lovely friends earlier, people hate anything metal that walks. They would shoot you and turn you into scrap metal faster than you can blink your fake eyelids. I'm armed and dressed like a soldier. Identifying myself as Hemlock carries weight. If they believe I have a claim on you, they shouldn't mess with you."

Block shook his head. "But ownership is wrong."

She's right. This is the way we have to do it.

"It's an act, Block. Pretend, for your protection."

Still, it didn't sit right with him. Even fake ownership perpetuated the idea that robots were people's property. Would there ever come a time when robots and humans could exist together and get along?

"If you're not with me on this," she said, "then we turn around and go back right now."

"I'm with you. Even though it's not right."

"Also, we have to be careful when we enter the city and meet Hemlock troops. I'll have to claim that I captured you. Shane's numbers have grown, and there'll be many who don't know you from before."

"Would you like to handcuff me and put Vacuubot on a leash?"

Her lip curled. "That's not a bad idea."

"I was joking," Block said quickly. "Absolutely no cuffs or leashes. That's the worst idea."

"It's definitely not a bad idea, but since I don't have cuffs, and I doubt a leash could keep your friend down, we can skip that part." She sighed. "You know I don't think like these people, right?"

Block wanted to believe her, but she'd fooled him in the past. She hadn't trusted him to take care of Wally and had given her to another human instead.

So he told Nova what she wanted to hear. "I believe you. I'll go along with it so we can complete our mission."

She nodded. That seemed to satisfy her, but Block calculated scenarios. Once he got Wally, he would ditch Nova, leave her with Shane while he and Wally returned to O'Hare escorted by Vacuubot.

The mouth of the tunnel entrance loomed ahead. This was where trains had descended underground and traveled into the heart of the city. Block prepared himself for the inevitability of human scavengers. They would likely be armed and dangerous. Would they bother listening to Nova, or would they shoot first? There was no other choice but to travel this route. Venturing above onto the city streets meant they'd be spotted by X's patrol drones and rounded up. The underground it was.

Nova halted and held her arm in front of Block. "Stay behind me." She gripped her rifle and switched on the headband flashlight. As they entered the dim tunnel, Block's night vision automatically switched on. Vacuubot hummed behind him, guarding the rear. Block's moisture indicator showed a humidity level of 75% and indicated noxious odors. The underground was no place to set up a hotel, that was for sure.

Nova pulled a bandanna from her pocket and held it to her nose. "Smells terrible."

Something big moved in the darkness ahead. Block's sensors showed orange heat patches.

Nova flinched and jumped back as her light shone on a water puddle that began to twist and move. "Rats!" She grabbed onto Block's arm.

On their previous travels, she'd had a terrible experience with rats when they'd ventured into an abandoned superstore. "Nova, would you like me to lead the way past the rats?"

Her eyes were wide, and she couldn't talk; she nodded violently.

"Okay, grab onto me from behind." Block shuffled forward, hoping the noise would scatter the rats. Nova latched onto his rear storage compartment where his cleaning equipment was embedded, keeping close.

Vacuubot zoomed past and launched toward the rats. They shone a spotlight on the huddle, causing the creatures to race in all directions, running past Block's boots before veering off. Block stamped his feet.

Behind him, "Oh crap, crap, crap."

"Stomp your feet so they don't climb on you," Block said.

Nova's boots clomped as if she'd suddenly taken up flamenco dancing. Twenty-three seconds later, the rats had cleared. Vacuubot messaged, *I'll lead the way from now on.*

"Nova, are you okay?" Block turned to face her. Her eyes were glassy, and her gaze darted around at the ground, the walls, and at her feet.

"The rats are gone now," he said. "You're safe."

But she gulped in air, hyperventilating. They didn't have time for this. The rats might return soon. If this was going to keep happening, they were in trouble.

"Come on." He guided her by the hand. *Let's go*, he messaged Vacuubot.

They continued through the dark tunnel. Water had pooled several inches deep in spots, and they kept on top of the tracks that were slightly elevated from the surrounding ground. Rats still scurried from their path but were fewer the deeper they went. The advancing human-robot trio scattered the rats into fissure-like cracks in the walls. Block hoped Nova wasn't really paying attention.

After a time, her breathing slowed, returning to normal. She let go of his back compartment. "I'm okay. I can walk on my own. I didn't know there'd be so many rats."

"They probably took over once the humans and trains went away."

"It's not helpful for you to keep talking about them," she said. "Anything else would be a better subject right now."

"Noted." But Block couldn't process what to say, so he kept quiet. Soon they would reach Shane, and it would be his chance to rescue Wally. He could barely believe he was back in Chicago, but it wasn't the way he'd envisioned a homecoming. He would have much preferred bringing Wally here to show her The Drake. Maybe even reopen the hotel in memory of Mr. Wallace. In his favorite scenario, he pictured Wally running up and down the halls, and playing catch with her at the lakeshore as she grew up there. Block was her caretaker, tutor, cook, and cleaner.

Her protector.

He'd analyzed this particular scenario hundreds of times, going in many possible directions, even throwing in a few random events. In each scenario, everything turned out okay. Wally grew up healthy and normal. Well, Block wasn't really certain what it meant to be normal for a human, but compared to humans like Shane, Wally turned into a fine person. She became a person like Mr. Wallace—a person who was kind—one whom he enjoyed being around.

Most importantly, Wally became an adult who was kind to humans, animals, and robots. Block and Wally kept in touch with Oxford, Maxwell, and even Cybel, who eventually warmed up and became a friend.

It was odd though. In all his scenarios, Nova didn't factor in, and he wasn't exactly sure why. He wanted her to, certainly. But she ended up going off on her own, living somewhere else out west. Chicago wasn't her home.

But it was Block's home, and it's where he would raise Wally.

This scenario would come true. He meant to keep his promise.

Chapter 16
I'd laugh if I could

After three hours plodding deeper into the abandoned train tunnel, they'd developed a rhythmic pattern: Vacuubot hovered in the lead, its light beam scanning left and right as the machine captured intelligence from a smaller drone sent ahead to scout; Block marched not far behind, occasionally glancing back at Nova who kept up fine, though she sometimes flinched at the sound of scampering rodents. But otherwise she was okay. And finally, in the rear, a second smaller drone flew backwards, looking out for threats.

"How much more of this?" Nova shivered from the twenty-degree temperature drop from when they'd started. In a few hours, night would fall, though below the surface, circadian cycles mattered less.

"We should soon reach the point where we can cross onto other tracks. This train line only ran from the airport to the business district and various points along the way, but other lines intersected that could take you along other city routes." Block knew they had to eventually travel farther east to reach the point on the river where Shane's troops were located. There were no underground train tracks that led to that section of the city, but he hadn't yet broken the news to Nova.

"Are you tired?" he asked. "Do you need to rest for the night?"

Her lips curled in a snarl. "In here? You've got to be kidding. I'd prefer sleeping in a prison toilet to camping in this rat-infested hole. I'll walk all night if we have to."

The rats and underground smells didn't bother Block; they couldn't physically damage him. This must, however, have been an awful experience for a human. It was no surprise they hadn't encountered any human scavengers, or any living things besides rodents.

Are you reading traces of any beings? he messaged Vacuubot.

There are signs that these tunnels have been well-traveled, but nothing recent.

How do you know?

Look. Observe, Vacuubot said. *You'll find clues.*

Block wasn't sure what the little drone meant at first, so he played around with his night vision settings, first lowering its sensitivity so heat flashes from Vacuubot and the drones faded from the edges of his vision. After a minute, he glimpsed outlines of objects among the pitch black: a wad of plastic, a battered license plate, and a tattered doll's head floated in the liquid muck next to the track. On the wall, a ladder that had led up to a manhole had been sheared off—the top third missing. It was as if someone had tried to cut off any means of escape from the tunnel.

Block kept going, observing quietly, grateful that Nova hadn't noticed these things. At least, she hadn't complained about them, and Block wasn't about to bring them to her attention.

A sign next to a door on the west tunnel wall said: *CTA Emergency Exit*. But the door had been barricaded with planks of heavy boards and sealed with dozens of nails haphazardly hammered through the sides.

Why is the door barricaded? Block asked Vacuubot privately, not wanting to rattle Nova.

Unknown, Vacuubot replied. *My logical assumption is that someone or something didn't want there to be exit options in this tunnel. That, or perhaps there's something beyond the walls that's worth hiding.*

Block thudded along, his boots splattering rotten pools of rainwater that had dripped down from the highway above.

"It's about as cheerful in here as Mach X's ass," Nova said.

Good one. I'd laugh if I could. Vacuubot beeped three times in rapid succession.

Nova halted. "What was that?"

"Vacuubot appreciates your humor," Block said. "That's its way of laughing, I suppose."

"Finally. At least someone gets me."

"What do you mean by that?" Block asked.

"In all our travels, you've never laughed at my jokes." Her shoulders loosened.

Good. This was getting her to think about something besides rats, at least. Often humans could be distracted easily by drawing attention to themselves. He made a note to point this out to Wally when she got older—one of the many lessons he would teach her.

"I didn't laugh, because technically I can't," he said. "Not real laughter. It's synthetic, designed to please humans."

"Well, you could appreciate it and give me props like little Vacuubot. Why is Vacuubot an 'it' anyway?"

"Vacuum CleanerBot programmers never assigned a gender. Vacuubot was an 'it' meant for cleaning and small jobs. The type of machine that would always be on the fringes, ignored and out of the way."

"You clean, but you got a gender."

She had a good point. "Yes, but I interacted with hotel guests."

"Oh, right. You told me a long time ago that humans prefer to know the gender when interacting with robots."

"Correct."

Vacuubot emitted a shrill beep, then buzzed. *Gender is stupid anyway.*

"What did it say?" Nova asked.

"Nothing useful."

"Ha. It's probably laughing at you," Nova said, and

Vacuubot beeped three times fast. "Ha, see!" She cackled and clapped once loudly—too loudly.

The noise echoed through the deep empty chamber, and Vacuubot hummed. *Something is ahead.*

Block slowed to a stop, causing Nova to bump into him. "Hey, what's—?" but Block held a finger up to silence her.

Her eyes widened and she raised her rifle. "What is it?" she mouthed.

Vacuubot's drone ventured forward to investigate, its body dark and sleek. Vacuubot extinguished the lights on its shell and undercarriage, and the only glow came from Nova's headband. She reached up with a frown and turned it off. "I don't like this."

What is it? Block messaged.

Another door is ahead. Barricaded like the one we saw earlier.

So? What's unusual about that?

There's noise coming from inside.

Nova tugged Block's arm. "Will you tell me what's happening?"

"A door has been barricaded, and there's noise coming from inside of it."

"So? Let's ignore it and keep going."

Vacuubot, is the door secure?

Yes. I don't detect a threat.

"Let's keep moving," Block said. "Keep your lights off just in case."

He reached behind, found Nova's hand. She clasped his tightly and shuffled along behind him.

Vacuubot flew slower now, its motor as quiet as possible.

Ten feet from the door, Vacuubot warned Block.

A faint clinking sounded from beyond the wall. The echoing made it hard to tell exactly where it was coming from. Block trusted Vacuubot's sensors to know what was happening. Maxwell's tune up had given the machine enhanced sensory abilities. The clinking kept a steady beat but grew faster the closer they got, despite how careful they were being.

Why would–? But before Block could finish, Vacuubot surged ahead and began scanning the door.

No! Block messaged. *That could be dangerous if someone has weapons or can detect—*

But Vacuubot spun and faced Block. *I know what's inside. Help me get this door open.*

Block backed up a step.

"Hey, watch it," Nova said. "I'm blind as a bat in here."

"This isn't a good idea," Block said.

If you won't help me, I'll do it myself, Vacuubot replied.

"What's not a good idea?" Nova switched her light on.

A pulsing red laser beam projected from Vacuubot's front display straight at the metal bolt that secured the door.

"What the—? Will you explain to me what's happening?" Nova swung her gun, checking behind them.

"I'm not entirely sure myself." Block stepped toward the door.

Stay away, Vacuubot warned. *You'll get hurt.*

"What's it doing?" Nova's voice was low and shaky.

"Slicing through that door apparently."

After ten seconds, the bolt melted and landed with a clunk on the ground. The door tilted open slowly, hinges groaning. Block's night vision revealed what had been clinking inside.

The metal hand of a robot appeared—outstretched, palm facing up. Then a round, steel head peeked out, a pair of small orange eyes glowing from its face plate.

"Help us," a soft voice pleaded.

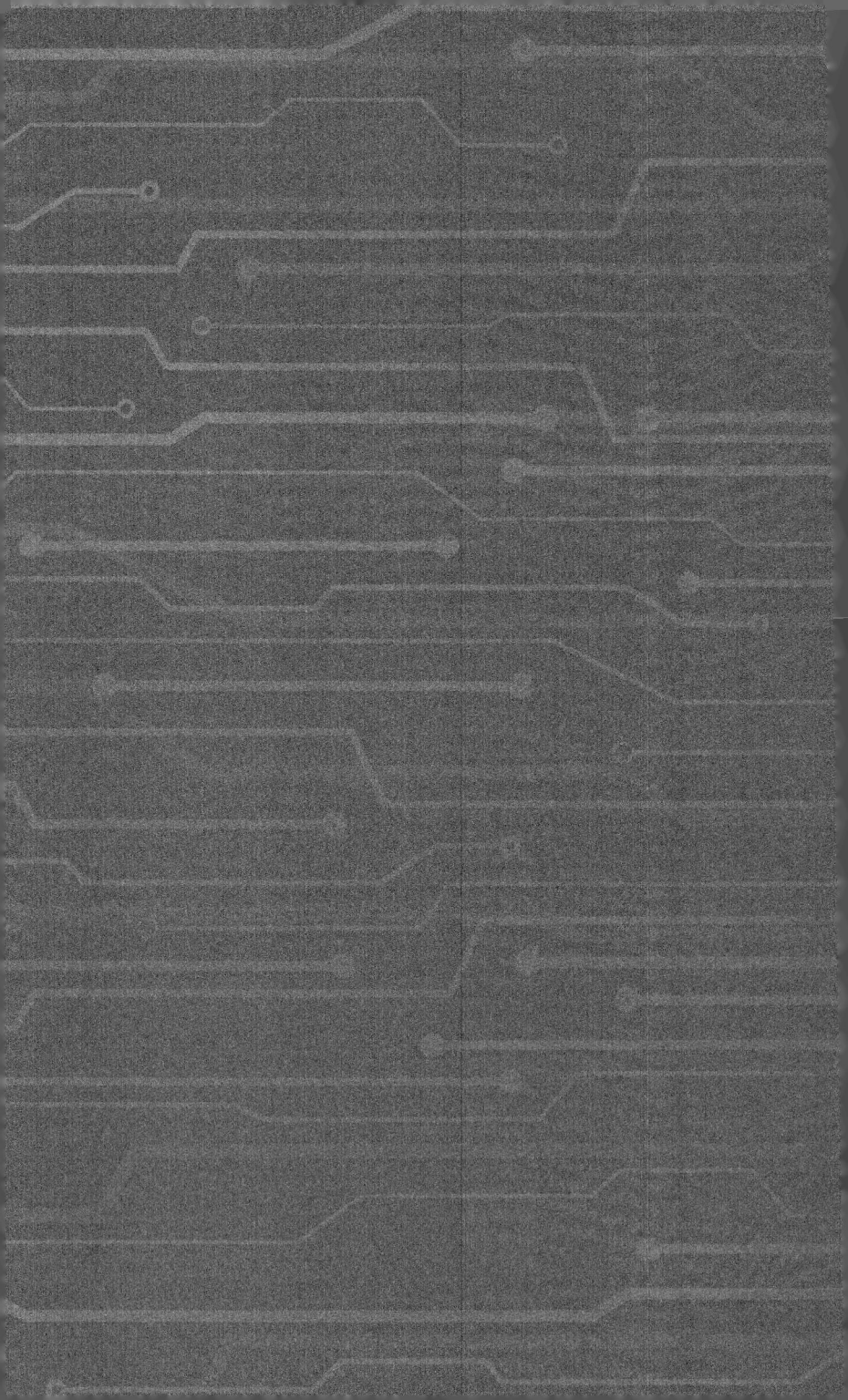

Chapter 17
You don't want to go there

They dragged two robots out of a closet-sized room that had once been a control area for train technicians. The first unit was a FactoryBot, a model similar to Maxwell's. It lay on the ground, struggling on its last energy reserves. Its companion—a SecurityBot—hadn't been so lucky. Its metal skull had been crushed in by something heavy.

Block fished out another of his fuel cocktails and hooked in the FactoryBot's tube. Powering back up took time; the robot wouldn't be at full strength for a while. Vacuubot hovered over the damaged SecurityBot, scanning the length of its body.

Any chance to salvage it? Block asked.

Several seconds passed, and they felt longer to Block, even though he knew that was logically impossible. Time was time and yet . . .

No. It's gone.

Nova stood by, clutching the gun barrel, while

Block crouched next to the weakened FactoryBot. "How would they have gotten in there?" she asked.

More like who bashed in the SecurityBot's head and left them to rot in a closet? This is not the work of SoldierBots, Vacuubot messaged.

"Someone hurt them and locked them inside," Block said.

"Why would anyone do that unless they were dangerous? Would these two be capable of fighting humans or SoldierBots?"

Block shook his head, and then Nova shined her beam inside the utility room. "I wonder if there are clues." She lingered in the doorway but didn't enter. "Freaking claustrophobic in there."

The FactoryBot stirred on the ground. "Can you speak?" Block asked.

"Thank you for the drink," it managed to say, its voice more masculine than feminine.

"You're welcome. We had to help, of course, do what we could. Who are you?"

"I'm Forge, a FactoryBot."

Block said, "I know someone who is almost exactly like you."

"Is she here?"

"He. No, he's not. I'm Block, an X4J6 CleanerBot."

Forge studied Block a moment. "I didn't realize what you were. I've never met a CleanerBot like you." His gaze traveled to Vacuubot. "Met plenty of drones though. Why hasn't this one shot at us?"

"The drone is with us," Block said. "We mean you no harm."

"Well then, I lucked out. Where is Thana?" Forge tried lifting his head but didn't get far. "I don't hear her."

"Is Thana your friend?" Block asked, knowing she must be, but wanting to delay the depleted FactoryBot from suffering another blow.

"Yes. She needs a drink too, if you don't mind. We've been in here a while." Forge stared up at Block. "I didn't think we'd ever get out."

Block lowered his synthetic eyelids. "I'm sorry. Thana expired. It was too late."

Forge raised up as if to sit but collapsed on his back.

"Help him sit, Block." Nova walked over and bent down at the robot's side. "With me."

Block helped her get Forge sitting up straight.

"Thana tried to defend me," Forge said. "I knew her from around the metalworks factory where I worked in the West Loop. She wasn't like the other SecurityBots. She was friendly, and sometimes we chatted privately. Gave each other news, sometimes gossip."

Nova's jaw clenched. "Who did this to her?"

"Humans. I didn't know them, of course. They were dressed in all black. They wore caps." Forge raised his hands in an awkward display of surrender. "Please don't hurt me," he said to Nova. "I won't hurt your robots. I am peaceful. I'll leave here without any resistance."

Nova recoiled. "I don't . . ." Her eyes couldn't meet Block's. She rose and paced away.

"Did I say something to offend her?" Forge asked. "I didn't mean to make her angry."

Block glanced at Nova who stood shivering twelve feet away. "No, you didn't. She doesn't own us. We're with her voluntarily. We're trying to get into the city."

"She doesn't own you. How can that be? She's human. Either they want to capture you or destroy you. That's how it is in Chicago. You don't want to go there."

"I'm sorry that was your experience." Block wanted to help Forge, but he was also keenly aware they had to reach the city in the early hours of the morning when the enemy patrols would be at their weakest. "Can you stand?"

"My energy reserves are at twenty-eight percent." Forge said. "I will try."

"Here, I'll help you." Block gripped Forge's left arm, and Vacuubot came over to assist by nudging Forge up on his right side. Together they got him standing.

"Why's she angry?" Forge asked, spotting Nova.

"She's not angry, just frustrated."

"Why do you want to go into the city anyway?"

"We're searching for someone. Someone who is extremely important, and we believe she's in Chicago. Held by Mach X."

And then Nova's voice was in Block's auditory

portal. "Quiet! What are you going to do, tell the robot our entire plan? Great. Just flipping great."

"Why would it matter?"

She pressed her hands on her hips. "What if it can still communicate with robots back in the city? What if they inform the SoldierBots?"

"I won't do that," Forge said. "I want to get out of Chicago, away from SoldierBots especially. They're as bad as the humans."

Forge has information we can use, Vacuubot messaged Block.

"What do you know about the SoldierBots?" Block asked. "Can you help us infiltrate them?"

Forge shook his head. "No. Thana and I kept as far away from them as possible. That's how we ended up down here underneath the city. We were trying to get out, but then a group of humans found us, hit Thana in the head with a crowbar for talking back, and locked us in. They said we could rot."

Nova hung her head when Forge said that last bit.

"Do you know if Mach X is in the city?" Block asked.

"Parts of X, maybe. I think. I heard X is mainly in New York City, but there's a rumor that X's core processor is in another location. One that's heavily guarded."

"Where? Could Mach X's core be here in Chicago?"

Forge said, "I doubt that. It would probably be in a very protected place."

"How do we find out where the SoldierBots are?"

"Just keep walking toward the city. They patrol, and if the drones don't find you first, scavengers and human rebels will get you eventually."

Block glanced at Nova. She nodded ever so slightly as if to say, go on.

"If you keep going and the humans find you, they'll take you prisoner and force you to work for them," Forge said. "That's what happened to me until Thana rescued me."

"What did they have you doing?" Nova asked.

"They made me assemble weapons and forced me to give information—anything I knew about how the SoldierBots worked. Anything to weaken them, intercept their communications. I wasn't the only one. There were others—WorkerBots, SecBots, CleanerBots."

"There were other CleanerBots?" Block asked.

Forge nodded. "If the robots didn't prove useful, didn't keep giving up valuable info, then the humans would scrap them. They made me take the dead robot parts and cast them into weapons. It was awful."

For the first time, Nova stared into Forge's faceplate. Her hands trembled, but Block couldn't tell if it was the temperature or something she was feeling inside. "Did these humans have a name? Any names that you remember or the name of their group?"

"Yes. First, I was in a group led by someone called Petra, but then they passed me over to a group called Hemlock."

Nova flinched. "Who was in charge there?"

"A woman named Kalin."

"A woman?" Nova's forehead wrinkled. "I don't know that name."

Forge shifted his gaze between Nova and Block. "You know of Hemlock?"

"Yes," Block said. "We're looking for them, in fact."

"She can go to them." Forge tilted his head at Nova. "But I'm warning you"— he looked at Block—"if you go there, it's termination for you and your drone."

"We can handle it," Nova said. "Hemlock knows me, or at least they used to. Did you hear of someone named Shane?"

"Let me review my memory logs." After half a second, Forge said, "Yes, the name Shane was mentioned, though I never saw the one named Shane. He was, perhaps, someone in charge but located elsewhere. Kalin was leader of the warehouse where they held me. She was the worst—everyone feared her. But after a while, she left, and someone named Michael was put in charge. He wasn't as diligent and that allowed me to escape—with Thana's help, of course."

"How long ago?" Nova asked.

"That was three days ago."

"What can you tell us about their location?" Block asked.

But Nova tapped his arm. "We don't need that." She pointed to the pin on her chest—the communicator that let her talk to Shane.

"Hey," Nova said to Forge. "I'm sorry the humans

did this to you and your friends. I'm sure they have their reasons. They're trying to arm themselves, attack Mach X. It's not easy . . ."

Vacuubot buzzed its disapproval. *Is this supposed to be an apology?*

"Anyway . . ." Nova couldn't look at Forge anymore. "Block, we need to go."

He knew she was right but what to do about Forge? The robot was in no shape to navigate the tunnels by himself.

"If you need rest," Forge said, "you could use the closet. Nobody should bother you in there. I can keep a watch out."

"We can't linger," Block said. "You'll have to go on by yourself in the direction we came from."

"Alone?"

"Yes. We didn't encounter any issues in the tunnel, though when you reach the above-ground tracks, be very cautious."

"There are snipers," Nova said. Vacuubot buzzed and beeped as if to reinforce the gravity of the situation.

"How can I survive if it's that dangerous? I have no place to go," Forge said.

"You can go where we came from"—Block pointed—"keep following the train tracks and you'll arrive—"

Nova yanked his shoulder. "No. Don't blow the hideout. What if this is a spy?"

Vacuubot made a slow, high-pitched whine.

Block spun to face Nova. "Look at him. His only friend had her head bashed in. Forge would have expired too if we hadn't come along. How could he be a spy?"

She gritted her teeth. "It's a bad idea. If people or bots find out about . . . the location, it puts the others in danger."

"There are others?" Forge asked.

Block paused, unsure of what to do. Forge was weak and unarmed, but they couldn't delay their journey in an effort to assist him. *What do we do?* Block messaged Vacuubot.

Nova's right that we have to get moving. Forge could wait in the closet for us to return.

That would put him at more risk. What if we don't come back this way?

"What's going on?" Nova asked. "Are you talking with Vacuubot behind my back? It's not fair that you two communicate and leave me out."

"I assure you we're not talking about you. We're weighing options. Our advanced processing capabilities make the analysis of scenarios quick. Much faster than you could—"

"Enough." She crossed her arms and huffed. "Hurry up and make a decision."

It's your call, Vacuubot messaged. *It's unlikely Forge would even make it to the airport without our help.*

It was true. Forge was a FactoryBot; his model wasn't meant to protect themselves or hike long distances. The route would be full of hardships.

Nova drummed her fingers on the side of the rifle.

Vacuubot fell silent. This seemed to be Block's decision, but why? He was no leader. And if he told Forge to head to the airport, Nova would be angry that he divulged the location. But if he sent Forge out anyway, the Bot was likely to be captured or shot by snipers.

He didn't want to make anyone mad—his relationship with Nova was already frayed, and he needed her cooperation to get in league with Shane again.

She had forbidden him to reveal the airport location, so he wouldn't.

"We have to get going," Nova said. "It's creeping me out being down here this long."

"Yes, I know," Block said. "Vacuubot will escort Forge to the hideout location."

Vacuubot rose up several inches and buzzed. *Are you sure?*

"No freaking way," Nova said. "We need that drone."

"Vacuubot will escort Forge and make sure he stays safe and reaches our friends. Note, I did not divulge the location."

Nova started to talk but bit back her words. She smirked. "You think you're so clever, don't you?"

"The goal is to help Forge reach safety without getting killed. In order to do that, he needs help, and Vacuubot is the best escort. I didn't tell him where he's going, so I didn't go against your wishes." Logic would dictate she should be satisfied with this arrangement, but she was so hopelessly emotional. Humans!

Block faced Vacuubot. "Take Forge back to where

we started. The others will receive him and take care of him. Forge, tell them that Block sent you, that we are okay, and we're continuing our mission."

"You're giving up your drone, for me?" Forge asked.

Nova scoffed. "Yeah, that's my question too. Block, you can't be serious."

"I am perfectly serious. My analysis says this is the best scenario in order for Forge to reach safety."

"What about our safety?" Nova asked.

"You have a rifle, and we're going to meet Shane whom you've been in touch with, haven't you?"

"Well, yeah."

"So, what's the problem? In fact, after hearing Forge's experience, the less they see Vacuubot, the better."

Nova's shoulders hunched, and she clutched the rifle as if for comfort. Just . . . fine. I don't care. Let's go. We've already wasted enough time here." She stomped through the muck, splashing water along the walls.

"Please, be safe," Block said.

"I don't know how to thank you," Forge said.

"Don't worry about it. Just reach our friends—robots like you. They'll take care of you. Vacuubot will shield you from any gunfire, but you have to be careful and try to go as quickly as you can." Block walked, but then remembered something. He reached into his thigh compartment. "Here. Take this." It was another pack of jet fuel cocktail, his second to last.

Vacuubot beeped low and long. *But you need that.*

So do the both of you. I'll find something else.

Be safe. Nova is unpredictable, but she means well.

Get Forge to safety and find us. You know how to locate me.

Will do.

Block jogged after Nova deeper into the tunnel leading toward the city. The knowledge that he was getting closer to Wally kept him going.

I'm coming, Wally.

Chapter 18
I don't mess up

Nova swung her head from side to side, flushing the tunnel from wall to wall with her light beam. Her pace was steady, but her steps were forced, undoubtedly, to scare any rats lurking in her way. Oddly, she didn't seem frightened anymore. Had her anger at Block cured her fear?

He'd tricked her, which had pissed her off. People didn't like being outsmarted by robot logic, especially not someone as confident as Nova.

But was it actually trickery? It had been a technicality, actually—Vacuubot was equipped to guide and protect Forge and get him to O'Hare safely. Nova, of all people, should understand it was the most sensible path, but she was more concerned with her own safety, or that losing Vacuubot meant less chance their mission would succeed.

"You'll tell me if we need to turn or something, right?" she called over her shoulder.

"Of course. We go straight for another mile."

She halted and spun, facing him. "Let's get something straight. No more playing me like that."

"Like what?"

"You know damn well what you did back there. Don't play naïve robot. I know you too well."

Block waited for her to call him more names, but she stared into his face display, and—there was no rational explanation for this—it made his circuitry feel exposed. "I'm sorry," he said. "It's just that you said, 'Don't tell Forge about the hideout.' You never said, 'Don't send Vacuubot to help Forge get to the hideout.'"

She kept staring. Talk about an awkward silence—thirteen whole seconds.

Finally, she broke. "I'm trying to help you, Block. You and Wally. You think I want to go suck it up and ask Shane for help?" She contorted her lips, then blew a stilted breath. "I've never gone back to someone. It's humiliating."

Block hadn't considered that she didn't want to see Shane again. "So, you won't get back together with him?"

"No. Of course not. Things ended between us, and not in a good way. Me going back is like"—she shook her head—"admitting that I messed up. And I don't mess up. Ever."

Block had archived memory evidence of several times she'd made mistakes, but he didn't bring it up.

Instead, he said, "I am grateful for your help. I couldn't go into the city without you."

That was apparently the right thing to say because the harsh edges around her mouth softened. "We have to act like a team. You can't play me or trick me like you did back there. If you're going to use your logic machine powers, use them for good, not to get something past me. Do you understand?"

Block nodded. He'd have to add another filter to his logic processor—a 'not tricking Nova' test.

"Because it's going to be dangerous," she said. "It's more than just Shane's people. You heard what that robot said. I'll be the only thing standing between you and…"

"I understand."

They followed the narrow tunnel and reached a second set of rail tracks that diverged.

"Which way?"

"Left," Block said after scanning the map Vacuubot had beamed him. "In 11.3 minutes, we'll reach an old underground station. It's a big one."

"Thanks for the heads-up. How big?"

"The station was a crossing point where people could get off and switch to other train lines."

"Where are we in the city right now?"

"South of the Chicago River and entering what used to be the Loop."

"Why did they call it the Loop?"

"It's shaped like a loop I suppose. There's a high

probability that there will be activity ahead—probably humans."

"Let me do the talking, got it?"

"Got it." In fact, Block was very comfortable with letting her to do the talking. Shane's troops had never liked him. They weren't like hotel guests who had been pleasant and relaxed, usually because they were on vacation or doing something fun. But the city was not fun anymore. Not when it was at war.

Nova ceased stomping her boots and treaded lightly, so Block mimicked her, and after several minutes, they slowed. A glow came from ahead and voices echoed across the walls. The aging brown concrete walls gradually changed to walls with aging pale blue and white tiles. These had once been Chicago's city colors.

Nova raised a finger to her mouth, though he didn't need the warning; often humans did the obvious thing. She was taking a big risk to help him find Wally. Had she been a robot that only followed logic, she wouldn't have helped at all.

But some part of her—maybe the emotional side that lacked rationality—had decided to help.

They crept closer, and a man wearing dark jeans and a long-sleeve black shirt lingered near the edge of the platform where passengers used to board. An assault rifle was slung casually over his shoulder. Nova craned her head for a better view and whispered, "There's three of them, maybe more."

Block waited for her to lead their advance, but she

waited a full minute. Her sweat level had increased, and she ran her slick hands across her rifle. What was she waiting for?

After thirty more seconds, Block tugged her sleeve. "What are you doing?" He said it as low as possible, but she yanked her arm away, and that made Block stumble back and his elbow struck the tiled wall with a clunk.

The man with the gun jerked his head and grunted. "Who's there?" he yelled into the dim tunnel. Block and Nova pressed against the wall, out of view.

Another voice shouted, "Someone out there?"

Nova said, "Stay put" to Block. Then she pressed away from the wall, toward the guards, hands raised in surrender. "Please, don't shoot. I mean no harm."

"Whoa. Stay where you are!" shouted a woman.

Nova halted, her arms trembling enough for Block to register.

"Hands up where I can see them," the woman said. "Higher!"

Nova raised her arms, as if reaching for the platform edge itself. "Please, don't shoot. I'm traveling to . . . h-here for a reason." Block had never heard her stammer before. He peeked around the corner.

"Shut up!" the woman said. The male guard was shorter with a patchy beard. He kept glancing at the woman who had long, sepia braids and was clearly in charge.

"Fred, go tell Pete and Vera to guard the other incoming routes. There could be more with her."

Fred raced away.

"I'm alone," Nova said. "I mean— uh . . . nobody's coming that way."

"So, you're not alone?"

Nova hesitated too long. The guard took a step forward, closer to a clear shot. "Tell me who you are and who's with you, or I shred you into spaghetti in the next five seconds."

"I'm looking for Hemlock. Shane Fletcher. My name is Nova, and I have his permission to travel here."

The woman blinked at mention of Shane's name. "Are you alone?"

"Not exactly," Nova said, now visibly shaking. Block had never seen her this nervous before.

"Give me a straight answer, or I don't care if you're the Queen of England, your ass is going down."

"I'm with . . . a robot"—the woman flinched and shifted her rifle's aim—"but it's just a CleanerBot." Nova forced a laugh. "Completely harmless. It's not even armed." Nova jerked her head at Block, beckoning him to reveal himself in the dim light coming from the platform.

He came forward with arms raised.

"Why do you have it?" the guard asked. "Why not blast its CPU?"

"Shane wants it."

"Why on earth would our Commander want a useless Scrapper?"

Our Commander. These were Hemlock people?

"He didn't tell me why. Said it has something he needs." Nova didn't stutter at all now. Was it because she was so good at lying? "Did he not mention that I would be arriving? Nova Kincaid."

The woman hesitated. Voices came from the far end of the platform, ricocheting off the walls. Fred returned, and someone else was with him. She walked with authority, and the braided woman's arms stiffened when she spotted her.

The woman was tall, with cropped blonde hair that had been shaved on one side, and her eyebrows were arched and thin. She marched to the edge of the platform—so close, the tips of her polished black combat boots poked over.

"Nova, I've been expecting you. I'm Kalin."

Chapter 19
All your old friends are there

Kalin stared down at Block. "What's with the Scrapper?"

Fred gave Nova a hand up onto the elevated train platform. "That's Block," Nova said. "Shane knows him."

Kalin's lips twisted like she had a joke on the tip of her tongue. "Shane said you have a way with robots." Then she stood by, watching as Nova helped Block up from the tracks. He only managed to get one knee up onto the five-foot-tall platform. Nova had to pull back with all her weight, dragging him until he fell over onto his side awkwardly, but at least he was on their level.

Kalin loomed over him, staring with a grimace before she spun on her heels. "Let's go."

They climbed a flight of stairs into a dilapidated building lobby. Fred stayed behind while Dee, the braided woman, trailed behind Block and Nova. She scowled at them with suspicion.

They exited through glass doors and emerged onto an empty city street. Block glanced up, hoping to glimpse city towers, but a tarp stretched all the way across the street from one building to another. Kalin hurried across the street, and Dee shoved Block in the lower back. He stumbled forward, nearly toppling over.

Nova spun and got in her face. "Hey! Don't push him like that."

"I'll do what I want," Dee said, grasping her rifle.

Kalin glared at them from the next building's main door. "Get out of the street," she ordered. "Now."

Nova walked close to Block as if protecting him as Kalin led them across another lobby. "There's something you have to understand," she said. "We can't be in the streets. We risk attack out there."

"Do the SoldierBots know you're here?" Nova asked.

"Undoubtedly. Yet so far they've put up with us, that is, when we stay out of sight. They're like a hive mind. They react to forceful leadership, and as far as we can tell, Mach X does not have a strong leader in Chicago."

Block thought about Oxford and how great of a leader he'd once been. Would the SoldierBots have listened to him?

"So, be a good friend of Shane's, and don't put us at risk." Kalin grinned at Nova. "Got it?"

"Yeah. Got it." Block recognized the sound of irritation deep in Nova's throat.

They worked their way through a maze of underground pathways that had been built to let city workers roam between buildings during the frigid Chicago winters.

"Why wouldn't the SoldierBots be down here?" Nova asked.

"They don't need to bother. Temperature certainly doesn't affect them." Kalin arched an eyebrow at Block. "When we first arrived, there were vagrant robots in these underground pedways. Weak ones like your friend there—holdovers from restaurants, buildings, and hotels. We figured the SoldierBots ignored them since they're harmless."

Nova nodded.

"What do you think?" Kalin whirled and faced Block.

"What do I think about what?"

"You've been listening to our conversation. You can even play it back in split seconds if you want to." Kalin was intimidating. Forge had said she'd been in charge at the warehouse where he was held, that she was feared. Block could understand why, and from the way she acted, she knew a lot about robots too.

"It's true that the SoldierBots think robots like me are harmless." A glance at Nova's clenched jaw told him not to say much. "They make fun of CleanerBots. So, if they assume that's all that's down here, they wouldn't care. You're right."

"Hmm." Kalin chewed her lip. "You're more advanced than the other CleanerBots I've seen. When were you made?"

"I don't remember," Block said too quickly.

"Don't lie to me." Kalin circled behind Block, pushed his head forward, and inspected the serial ID tag and manufacturing date on the back of his neck. "Less than two years old. Interesting. Where did you work?"

"A hotel."

"Which one?"

He didn't want to tell her. Something about her flagged his threat indicator. She meant harm, but he didn't know how exactly.

"The Prairie." It was a fine hotel but not nearly as nice as The Drake.

She smirked, but his answer seemed to satisfy her. They continued for another twelve minutes before arriving at Marina Towers. It was located along a popular pre-Uprising tourist area of the river. Boat sightseeing tours often gathered here to board passengers.

A long staircase led to a basement level where armed personnel guarded the entrance. Inside was the old marina where boats had docked along the river. Long sheets of tarp had been strung up to obscure the view onto the river, its flaps shuddered against the outside wind.

"Welcome to the command hub," Kalin said.

Just like in the gymnasium back in the Colorado elementary school, women and men busied themselves over maps, blueprints, old computers, and tablets. Stacks of ammunition and weapons lined a wall on one side. Two women guarded the supply while others waited in line.

Shane stood at a table in conference with a tall man wearing a black cap. Block was used to Shane looking as if he'd gotten bad news, and this time was no different—his arms were crossed, and he wore a frown. His eyes caught their movement as they entered the room, and he seemed to freeze as a flicker of a smile flashed, then disappeared when he spotted Block.

Nova turned to Block. "Stay here. Let me talk to him." She walked over, and Shane dismissed the tall man. Nova kept her arms at her sides, her body language stiff. They were in conversation, but with the number of people talking and the flapping tarp, the noise level was far too high for Block to listen in.

"What do you think they're talking about?" Kalin asked him.

Logic told Block the less he said to her, the better. His threat indicator thrummed, which was never a good sign.

"She needs something," Kalin continued. "Shane hates nothing more than a weak person with nothing to offer him."

Block said nothing. Nova had her back to them and was talking a lot while Shane listened.

"Maybe she's going to offer you up as payment. I hope so. I would so enjoy interrogating you." Kalin nudged his elbow. "Pulling you apart piece by piece."

He wished Nova would hurry.

"What do you think, *Block*?" She mocked his name,

emphasizing the hard sound at the end. "Do you want to come see my lab? It's loads of fun. All your old friends are there."

She was hideous. Worse even than the soldiers-in-training had been at the Hemlock survivor camp. Forge had been lucky to escape.

A voice came from behind, one Block recognized. "Well, I'll be."

Block swiveled his head to confirm his disappointment. Yep. "Hello, Pete," he said.

Kalin nodded in greeting, and Block registered a twitch of apprehension cross Pete's face.

"You know this CleanerBot?" she asked.

"Yeah. Nova kept him in the basement back in Colorado."

"Really?" Kalin rocked on her heels. "Kept him in the basement like a rat?"

Pete glanced around and spotted Nova. "Yeah, she had a soft spot for this Scrapper for some reason."

Kalin scowled. "How weird. And for some odd reason, Shane still has a soft spot for *her*." She gazed their way, narrowing her eyes.

"Why are you back?" Pete asked Block. "Thought you were supposed to go off and protect the baby girl. Keep it away from Mach X."

Kalin crossed her arms. "What do you and Nova want anyway? I'm quite interested to find out."

Block was cornered. Nova was supposed to handle all the talking. He hadn't planned anything to say, and they hadn't practiced or anything. His threat indicator pulsed with a warning. If he let something stupid slip out, Nova would be furious.

He could ruin everything and miss his chance to find Wally. She could be anywhere in the city.

He glanced at Nova, still deep in conversation with Shane.

"Well?" Kalin asked. Then she rolled her eyes and said to Pete, "This may be our only chance to get the CleanerBot alone, while Shane's distracted."

Pete's frown turned into a mean little smile. "Let's take him to the pit."

Chapter 20
Base of a skyscraper

Pete grasped Block's neck and pushed him forward, not even bothering to threaten Block with his gun. The man had no fear of retaliation by a CleanerBot, apparently. Block didn't like the sound of whatever the pit was. He considered shouting, trying to alert Nova, but by the time Pete and Kalin had shuffled him out of the command room, it was too late. Nova was out of earshot and completely distracted.

They shoved him along a steep path onto an underground road in a part of the city he'd never been before. Three soldiers with guns sat on the sidewalk playing a game of cards and passing a flask. As Kalin and Pete approached, they scrambled to their feet.

"At ease," Kalin said.

The men gaped at Block, and one of them said, "Hey, I know that Rust Bucket. It used to mop the floors."

Pete grinned at them. "Want to have some fun at the pit?"

"Hell, yeah," one of them said, but the man who recognized Block hesitated and glanced at the door leading to the command hub.

"What's the matter with you?" Pete asked. "Fine, stay behind."

Block pumped his legs forward as Pete prodded him from behind. His threat indicator flashed at 95.5% Where was Nova?

Kalin marched ahead, and Pete kept pace. Block ran scenarios, including a few where he purposely stumbled and fell, but it wouldn't matter because Pete would drag him up. There was no way to escape, and besides, if he did, they'd probably shoot him.

Finally, they surfaced above ground where the muted sky was a murky gray black. Block glimpsed his Chicago—the looming towers with flecks of artificial light glimmering through windows, though not so many as before the Uprising. Now, the lights came from SoldierBots instead of humans. Block's appreciation of his home city still lingered, but the allure had faded.

He wondered about being outside—about SoldierBot drones, which Kalin had warned about—but judging by her smile, he concluded it wasn't a concern at night. That, or she just didn't care anymore.

After a minute of trampling through patches of uncut dry grass and overgrown prairie weeds, a gaping hole appeared in the earth.

"Behold," Kalin said.

Pete shoved Block toward the edge, his strong hands coiled around Block's neck so they forced his gaze down.

Block's night vision kicked on in time to register that the pit was as tall as four or five houses stacked together. The hole's circumference matched that of an Olympic-sized pool and had been perfectly measured and cut as if a gigantic drill had descended from the heavens to carve it out.

"What is it?" Block asked.

"It was the base of a skyscraper, but abandoned long ago," Kalin said.

"Now it's the pit." Pete cackled, and the two soldier tagalongs joined in. "What's down there?" Even Block's night vision sensory camera couldn't see all the way to the bottom.

"Why don't we throw you down there and see what you find?" Kalin asked, eliciting a jeer from the soldiers.

"Great idea. Now where is that rope?" Pete let go of Block's neck and searched the ground, kicking away dirt and grassy patches. After twenty feet, he found what he was looking for. A twisted, fraying old rope.

One end of the rope was a noose, which Pete looped over Block's head and tightened around his neck.

Kalin blew Block a kiss. "Have fun down there."

Pete kicked him over the edge. Block's arms pinwheeled as he struggled for balance, falling backward into the gigantic hole. The rope's slack ran out and tightened, ramming Block's body into the pit wall.

He bounced—hard—three times until he reached out and grabbed on to something in the wall in a desperate attempt to steady himself. His night vision revealed his anchor—an outcropping of moss and plants that were growing from inside deep cracks. He scanned slowly left and right—more of the same random vegetation. No telling how old the pit was, but he guessed five years or more; it had been at least three years before the Uprising since any new towers had been erected in Chicago. Much of the urban construction money had dissipated when the first signs of robot discontent had begun, when the wealthy investors had panicked and pulled their funding.

He hung eighteen feet deep into the pit. Above him, Pete, Kalin, and the soldiers laughed as they shone flashlights down and blinded his night vision.

"How's it hanging down there?" one of them called.

"Don't look down," Kalin said.

But he did look down, away from the light. Another fifty feet down, he spotted at least a dozen battered robot bodies.

Oh no. He would be the next dead robot. Coming here was the worst idea ever. They would drop him down in this pit, and Nova would never find him.

The rope moved slightly, and a hammering rang out from above. One of the men spit, and Block ducked out of the way to miss it. A long moment passed, and then the voices disappeared. Block hung, suspended by his neck, halfway down a pit that was full of dead, probably tortured, robots. And Nova didn't know where he was.

Wally, I have failed you. Block was sure this was his end of life. Certainly, the humans had tied him here and probably planned to return in the middle of the night to torture and terminate him. Or maybe Kalin was holding him here temporarily before moving him to her lab where she would make good on her promise to tear him apart piece by piece.

He grasped at the pit's wall, and his fist squished into a mound of wet dirt. He left his metal hand where it had landed, letting it get moist and soiled. For once, he didn't care about being dirty. There was no urge to clean.

If he ever got himself out of this situation, he resolved to get tougher. He would ask Nova and Oxford to teach him fighting skills. He would finally learn to shoot a gun.

He would not let Wally grow up to be a victim.

Over two hours passed. Nova would have known he was missing unless Kalin had made up a lie about him. Was Shane in on the plan? If so, maybe he'd told Nova that Block had left on his own—that he'd abandoned Nova.

Or maybe Nova was back with Shane after realizing she still loved him and would now join sides with him. Maybe she'd forgotten about Block entirely.

Block tried to climb up the pit's wall by sticking his feet and hands into the cracks, but the crevices were slippery, and he kept losing his grip.

He looked down at the dead robots and tried to determine what they had been—a few SoldierBots, FactoryBots, and something that looked very much like Teena the older model CleanerBot that had worked at The Drake with him so long ago. He couldn't be sure if it was actually her since the model was fairly common among the downtown hotels.

It hurt to see one of his own models down there. Why were the humans so cruel? Yes, robots were entirely different, yet they had feelings too. He wondered for an instant whether Wally might be better off away from other humans.

Block let go of everything, cut off power to his arms and legs, and hung like a sad doll.

Why bother trying to escape? What was the point? Everything was against him.

Was it? The little bit of power still circulating in his logic processor computed that no, not *every*thing was working against him. That was a mathematical impossibility.

He would not give up. Wally was out there, and she needed help. He was the only one fighting for her.

A light shimmered far above, visible in his periphery. He looked up at the sky, expecting a shooting star or some other cosmic oddity.

The light dimmed for several seconds and then brightened as it got closer. The beam changed from white to blue, and an engine hummed as it hovered directly over the pit's opening.

A SoldierBot drone, it must be. Any minute, they

would seize him. Of course, Kalin and Pete had left him there to be captured. Nova might never know what happened to him.

Block scrambled to hold onto the wall as a spotlight searched the sides of the pit, but his metal hands were too slick; they clutched at soggy pieces of soil and missed.

He swung on the rope, helpless as the search beam found him. He was exposed.

Chapter 21
Stopping is for weaklings

The spotlight fixated on him, then flicked off. The drone was coming down into the pit. So, the Soldier-Bots would execute him remotely. Perhaps that was for the best. A quicker end.

But a comforting, oddly familiar vibration greeted his sensors. The robot beeped and buzzed four feet above.

Block recirculated power to his limbs, then jostled his arms and legs. He shouted, "Vacuubot, I'm here," and then he remembered he didn't need to talk. *I'm here in this craterous hole.*

I see you. Vacuubot hovered level to Block. *Can you get out?*

No. I tried to climb but I keep slipping.

Where is Nova?

I have no idea. The humans here are cruel. Nova doesn't even know I'm down here I don't think. I'm uncertain.

Vacuubot buzzed. *Grab onto my shell. I'm going to fly you out of here.*

Can you support me? I weigh three times as much as you.

We'll find out, Vacuubot said.

Vacuubot released three drones, one of which soared up and out of the pit. *It will pull the rope from above.* The other two flew underneath Block's feet.

"What are you doing?" Block reached for the wall and dug his steel fingers into a damp crack.

Focus, Vacuubot said. *Place your feet on the drones' backs. They will help you.*

Block's stiff legs vibrated as the drones tucked themselves under his heels and levitated.

Now grab on to me with both arms.

There was a 38.8% chance this would work, but it was better than the alternative—adding to the heap of dead robots at the pit's bottom. He hooked his left arm on top of Vacuubot's armored shell, twisted, and grabbed on with his right arm. The noose around his neck loosened as Vacuubot and the foot drones ascended a few inches at a time.

But what if Pete and Kalin were up top, waiting and watching? They could return at any moment, finish Block off, and worse—hurt Vacuubot. "Wait. Leave me here. I don't want you to get hurt."

I'm not leaving you.

How strange that Vacuubot was the only one who could help him, and yet, Block hadn't saved Vacuubot when it was in danger.

They rose another ten inches, and Vacuubot's power unit strained. The drone under Block's left foot was weaker than the right, so his legs grew lopsided on the way up, making him shift his weight to stay balanced. He wondered if the sensation was similar to riding a skateboard.

Vacuubot must have been using practically all of its energy; Block wished the rescue process was faster. They'd gone four feet higher—fourteen more feet to ascend—when Block said, "Let's stop here so you can reset."

Stopping is for weaklings. We keep going.

Block leaned his head back, studying the pit's rim. "I have an idea." He grabbed the rope above with his right hand, taking much of his weight off Vacuubot and the drones under his feet.

"I saw this in a movie once. Hold on five seconds." Vacuubot waited as Block grabbed the rope with both hands to support his body. "It was *The Princess Bride* when Andre the Giant climbed the Cliffs of Insanity on a rope. He had to support the weight of four other people: Buttercup, Westley, Inigo, and Vizzini."

You don't have the strength to climb the rope all that way.

"Maybe not, but if you and the drones push me from below, perhaps that will help and not drain you of so much energy."

Block slowly raised himself up, one fist at a time like he'd seen in the movie, even though his CleanerBot arms weren't equipped to support his entire body.

I don't like this. But Vacuubot flew down anyway and hovered underneath Block's feet with the other drones. *How hard do we push?*

"Let me get used to this. I can only go so fast." He switched his grip again and again. "Hey, I'm getting better at this. You can push slightly harder."

And it was better. They didn't travel quite as fast as when Vacuubot was lifting him, but it was fast enough and less worrisome for Vacuubot's energy reserves. Foot by foot they climbed, and soon Block was only five feet from the top. "Almost there."

In the distance came a high-pitched shout. "Block!"

He jerked his head. That was Nova's voice calling out, though she sounded far. "Vacuubot, send a drone. It's Nova."

One of the drones surged out of the pit toward the sound of her voice. Block climbed the rope another foot, then looked up as Nova leaned over the edge of the pit.

"Holy crap! What happened?"

"I could use some help," he said.

She scrambled away from the edge, grabbed the rope, and yanked it to raise him from the pit until he'd nearly reached the top. Then she dragged him up and onto solid ground. Block lay on the bare soil, energy reserves low from the extra processing, added threat analyses, and the effort from climbing.

Vacuubot landed at his side, beeping and buzzing in dismay. *Tell her what happened.*

Nova panted. "Are you okay?" She shook her head at the pit, then at the noose around his neck, which she loosened and removed. "Who did this?"

"They did. Shane's people."

"What? But . . . Shane would never give orders to hurt you, not when I'm here to protect you."

So much for Nova's idea of protection. "It was the woman named Kalin and Pete from Colorado."

She balled her fists. "That bastard. I'll kick his scrawny little ass. And Kalin? She sat beside me at dinner and said you'd gone to a spot where there was gasoline and oil to fuel up. I believed them . . . and the whole time she was grinning like a creepy carnival clown." Nova scrambled up. "I need a gun."

Block rolled onto his back. "Please don't go causing trouble right now."

"Why not? Look what they did to you! Put a noose on you and hung you down into that pit—I mean, what's even down there?" She approached the edge and trained her flashlight beam at the bottom. "Is that . . . ?" She came back and crouched beside him; her voice was strained. "I'm sorry you had to see that."

"Me too. Hard to believe anyone would do something like that."

"These people . . . Shane is different than before."

"What happened when you talked to him? Does he know Wally's location? Will he help us locate her? That's all I care about—getting Wally, and getting out of here."

"I know. Me too." She sat beside him, drew her knees to her chest, and switched off the flashlight. "He says there's a heavy contingent of Mach X troops, centralized in the old Sears tower."

"That's the tallest skyscraper in Chicago. I've never been, but I've seen it many times. Everyone knows it."

"Right, and it's a massive tower that's heavily guarded. Shane has very little information about what's even inside."

"Shane believes Wally is there?"

"The only information they have is based on what Kalin has managed to extract from two SoldierBots they captured."

Block knew extract was code for torture.

"Apparently there's a wipe out chip inside the SoldierBots, so when their sensors detect an enemy threat, it scrubs their memory archives clean. The way Shane described it, Kalin is very good at extracting the intel *before* that happens. She's the only one who can do it."

"I don't like her."

"You and me both. Like I said, Shane's different now. Now he has this weird entourage—these advisors who are grooming him for a war against Mach X. He's seeking power . . ."

"Does he want to help us?" Kalin had hinted that Nova would need to offer something valuable.

"He listened to me, at least." Nova paused. "But he's so influenced by these people now. This Kalin. I don't know where she came from but . . ."

Focus her, Vacuubot messaged.

"Will Shane help us?" Block asked.

"I said that we want Wally, and in exchange I would help him infiltrate the tower." She shut her eyes. "But it wasn't good enough. He said he has more soldiers now, he doesn't need one more, especially one who—in his words—disobeys orders."

This did not sound promising.

"To hear him talk like that, after all we've been through . . . after our relationship. But I guess I'm partly to blame for the way I left." She hugged her knees and dropped her chin. "We went around and around, and eventually he agreed to help."

"He did? Why?"

She sighed, and Block recognized that she'd done something he wouldn't approve of. He knew her operating patterns now—she left little clues like sighing and going silent.

"I told him you could help. That you know how to hack into other robots, not only drones, but more advanced robots."

"But I destroyed the device that let me do that."

"It turns out he has one of those hack boxes. They haven't used it yet. It's untested, but they believe it'll work."

Vacuubot emitted a low angry beep, and Block sat up straight. "Why don't they use it? Why me?"

"Shane and Kalin believe it would work better for another robot to control a SoldierBot who can get us past the guards and entry gates, into the tower. And . . . since you've done it before on a Mech . . ."

She told! Vacuubot said.

Block's threat indicator flashed, and he suppressed it, annoyed. "How did Shane find out that I had used it on Oxford?"

Her fingers dug into her knees. "I let it slip. I'm sorry."

Block's energy reserves had increased, and he stood.

This idea is terrible, Vacuubot said.

I know. Block walked away.

"Wait." Nova scrambled after him. "If we do this—if you can pull this off—it means you get Wally. Shane promised me, on his life, that he would let us take her, no interference. That was my condition."

"And you believe him?" Block didn't look at her, didn't want to see her emotive human face—no doubt a ploy to make him feel sorry for her.

Her voice was unexpectedly firm. "I believe him."

We shouldn't trust the humans. Remember what they did to you in the pit? Vacuubot messaged. *Nova's judgement is compromised. She had a romantic relationship with Shane, and humans do dumb things when they are in love.*

How do you know that?

I watched a lot of soap operas when my human owners didn't know.

Block was impressed by how much knowledge had been trapped inside Vacuubot's limited body.

Maxwell's modifications had allowed its exterior to catch up with the more sophisticated interior.

We shouldn't trust them, Vacuubot repeated.

But what other choice did they have than to work with the humans? Block and Vacuubot trying to sneak into the tallest skyscraper in the city without being scrapped by legions of armed SoldierBots?

"Shane will make good on his promise. I'll hold him to it. He knows when I'm pissed—"

Block kept walking. "Save your breath. I'll do it."

Vacuubot buzzed angrily.

"You will?" Nova caught up to Block, energy surging in her voice. "Awesome. All right, now let's start to plan—"

Block halted and raised a steel index finger. "No. You've been calling the shots for far too long. I listened to you, and you led me to Hemlock, where there were no robots and you took Wally away."

She flushed. "Block, I—"

"Listen to *me,* for once. I let you keep me in that school with Shane and his awful soldiers. I let you keep Wally away from me when I could've been protecting her. Mach X attacked and killed so many." Block's fists clenched involuntarily, and a routine automatically started checking for an operating glitch. "And the worst part is I trusted *you* with Wally in the desert, and X got her."

Nova recoiled as if she'd been punched.

"I will do this one thing for you," Block said. "If this is Shane's payment for me to get Wally, then fine. I'll get his cruel, robot-killing soldiers into that building if that's what he wants. But then I'll take Wally away from here, and you and I are done."

She opened her mouth to speak, but only a funny, choking sound came out. He might've spied a tear, but he didn't care.

Chapter 22
A circuit loose

Block clutched the rectangular black box in his steel hands, weighing it and logging details he hadn't had time to assess in Arizona, where hacking into Oxford had been an accident. Now that he was supposed to intentionally use the device, his circuits jumped with spasms of nervous electricity.

He stood with his back against a wall, trying somehow to blend in with the concrete gray slab that comprised a city building. Next to him, Nova tried to slow her breathing. Observing them from the sky above, Vacuubot messaged, *Two SoldierBots around the corner, across the street.*

"Two targets close," Block relayed to Nova.

She edged toward the corner and glanced around it —fast—and flattened her back against the wall. "Targets identified." She narrowed her eyes at Block. "What now? You point the device at them?"

He fidgeted with the square, dense device. "That's basically how it worked last time. We have to pick one."

"Does it matter?"

"I don't know."

Hurry up, Vacuubot said. *I'm already getting pinged up here by other drones. They're no match for me though, and so far, I've been able to steer them away from your position.*

"The one on the left," Nova said.

"Why that one?"

"Because you said to pick one." She gritted her teeth.

"Okay. I need to point the device at it."

"Be my guest," Nova shifted and let him take the spot closest to the corner.

Block lingered for a moment, reminding himself that Wally was inside the looming tower. He hated this plan, but if it meant rescuing Wally, then it was worth it. He gripped the device in both hands, spun in view of the SoldierBots, and pointed the box. His finger clicked against the button like he'd done to hijack Oxford's operating system.

He wished he could hack a Mech instead of a single SoldierBot, but Shane wanted a stealthy approach.

The pair of SoldierBots were talking to each other and facing away, unaware of Block. They kept talking and . . . nothing changed.

Block pointed the device again and clicked, but the

two enemy robots kept talking. Block didn't know what to do. He just stood there.

"What's happening?" Nova whispered.

"Nothing. I don't think it's working."

Finally, a SoldierBot marched a few steps from the other one, then spotted Block.

"They see me," he told Nova. "Stay hidden."

The SoldierBot pointed out Block to its companion. They were sizing him up, registering his make and model. The second SoldierBot waved dismissively and turned away. Being a CleanerBot had its advantages.

But the SoldierBot who had first spotted him—the hacking target—approached Block, weapon pointed down because, after all, there was no need for a SoldierBot to feel threatened by a CleanerBot.

"Hello, there," Block ventured.

"CleanerBot, what are you doing in this area? It's a restricted zone."

"It is?" When being interrogated, 'play dumb' was Maxwell's advice. "I'm lost."

Maybe the device hadn't worked because Block hadn't been close enough. That, or maybe it didn't work at all. Nova had mentioned it was untested. If so, this plan was absolute lunacy.

"I don't care if you're lost, you don't belong here. Where did you come from?"

"Me?" Block nonchalantly tried pressing the hacking device again at his side, but the SoldierBot's demeanor didn't change.

"I'm looking for someone. Someone who might have a human child. Have you seen any around?"

"Aren't you a strange CleanerBot? Does your threat indicator not work? Don't you see I'm armed?" He laid a heavy carbon-fiber hand on his rifle. "None of us will hesitate to shoot you. We're looking for more scrap so we can make more Bots like me. This is Mach X territory." He gestured at the tower. "Stay out. I don't care where you go."

Most days, Block would have already been racing away, heading out of sight. No CleanerBot with standard self-preservation coding would consider challenging or questioning a dangerous SoldierBot.

But today was different. Today, Wally's life was at stake.

"But what about the child that's here? Have you seen her?" Block was pushing it.

"You must have a circuit loose in your processor," the SoldierBot said. "Get out of here, and if I catch you again, I'll shoot you in the CPU." The SoldierBot stomped away.

As he walked away, Block raised the device one more time, pressed the button, then turned and ducked around the corner where Nova waited with her gun drawn.

"That was flipping dangerous," she said. "Why did you prattle on? That thing almost shot you, and I would've had to intervene."

"He didn't almost shoot me. I'm just a CleanerBot.

A weakling to them. This device doesn't work." He held it out to her.

"What the . . . ? She told me it would work. Kalin probably made it up to get me out here and have me killed. She's after Shane, and she's jealous of me."

Block was about to tell her he didn't want to hear her romantic troubles when the SoldierBot rounded the corner. Nova flinched and aimed her rifle, inching back.

Block raised his hands. "Take me but leave her."

But the SoldierBot stood there, staring, so Block raised his hand slowly and waved it side to side. "Hello?"

"Hello," the SoldierBot said. The tonal personality it had spoken with before had been stripped; its voice sounded flat and monotone like Oxford's had been when Block had obtained control.

Block reached out and tapped an index finger on the SoldierBot's chest. It didn't respond. "Nova, the hack device worked."

But she didn't loosen the grip on her gun.

Block glanced around the corner of the building. The other SoldierBot waited there, on patrol.

Vacuubot messaged, *looks like you got the SoldierBot under control, but you need to hurry. There's some kind of drill or something happening on the south side of the tower.*

"What now?" Nova asked, her eyes darting to the hijacked SoldierBot.

"It's under my control. I should be able to command it to do what I want, but I have to be near it."

"Can't you control it remotely from out here?"

"No, it doesn't work that way."

"Well, the two of us can't just waltz into Mach X's Chicago compound. They'll kill us for sure."

"You they would kill, but I'm only a CleanerBot."

Her eyes widened. "What are you saying?"

"There's no time to argue." Block faced the SoldierBot, speaking with a calm confidence out of synch with his threat indicator. "Act like you've taken me prisoner. March me into the tower but heed my instructions. Tell the other SoldierBots that you found a CleanerBot, and you're taking me to your Commander."

"Understood," the SoldierBot said.

Nova grabbed Block's arm. "Are you serious? Going in there alone?"

"You wanted me to do a job. Go in and infiltrate the tower. Find the command room, plant the device that will knock out the drones and surveillance. Isn't that what Shane asked us to do?"

"Yes, but . . . "

"Then there's no question, and time is wasting. I will get the mission done, and then I'll find Wally."

Block faced the SoldierBot. "I'll walk in front of you while you aim your rifle at me. Wait. On second thought, I'm no danger so, push me ahead, no rifle. When the others make fun of my model, you'll join in. Is that understood?" Block nearly fell over; he wasn't used to giving anyone orders, much less a SoldierBot.

"Understood."

"You must take me to the communications hub and help me get inside."

"Understood."

"I'll be here waiting," Nova said. "Your back up when you need me." She slapped a magnet communicator onto his chest. It was a symbol he didn't recognize.

"It's something Hemlock gave me so we can communicate." She tucked a bud in her ear. "I didn't think we'd have to separate . . . the SoldierBot can take me hostage too—"

"No. They might kill you right away. Me on the other hand, I'm entertainment. They'll joke at my expense and probably put me to work."

Block turned to leave, and Nova rapped her knuckles on his back. "Please be careful."

He said nothing and walked ahead of the SoldierBot, not once looking back at Nova. He was only doing what Shane wanted so he could find Wally. Once he got her, he wouldn't come back for Nova. He could not risk her trickery again.

Eyes in the sky, please, he messaged.

You need to pass the one SoldierBot, then you'll encounter two more SoldierBots that guard the entrance to the tower. Normally there are more, but like I said, there is some training exercise happening another street away. You got lucky.

Good. At least one thing was going in his favor. Block stowed the device inside his thigh compartment.

He knew the device should be kept near enough for the range to penetrate the target. They approached the second SoldierBot, the one who'd waved at Block dismissively.

Her voice was feminine. "G5, why did you retrieve the CleanerBot? I told you to ignore it."

"I'm taking it to the Commander." G5 didn't quite sound his usual self, and Block hoped that wouldn't be too painfully obvious.

She said, "Why so serious? You don't have to turn it in. Use it for target practice if you want."

"I must take it to the Commander," G5 said.

She scanned Block. "It does look scrappy. Maybe Doc Blaze can do something with it. Soup up the CleanerBot and make it into some kind of missile launcher. But that's a lot of work. I'm not sure how you could ever improve on this model. Useless CleanerBot."

G5 emitted a tinny sound that was supposed to be a laugh.

"Are you glitching?" The second SoldierBot leaned in, inspecting her buddy.

Oh no. Earlier, Block should have told G5 to keep moving. If this other one sensed something was wrong . . .

She waved at the tower. "On you go. Get back soon. I'll cover for you while you're gone."

G5 pushed Block along in front of him. They were a hundred feet from the tower entrance when Block swiveled his head. "Keep us moving. No stopping for conversations."

"Understood."

"Also, you did well. Thank you." Weird time for his politeness programming to kick in.

G5 the SoldierBot paused three extra milliseconds as if struggling to process the command. "Understood."

G5 said nothing as they entered the tower lobby. Most Chicago residents and tourists had referred to the building as Sears despite multiple name changes over the years. Perhaps it should now be called Mach X tower? No. That would never sit right with Block, and if Mr. Wallace had seen what was happening to his beloved city, he would have been sad.

Block would try to make things right in his own small CleanerBot way. Getting Wally back was step one.

He wished he'd asked Maxwell to put a tracking device on her. Block wanted to kick himself for not having calculated the idea back in the desert.

Next time would be better. He wouldn't repeat the mistake—Wally would get chipped.

A set of elevator doors stood on the south side of the building. The hack job was still working. G5 was under Block's control—as much control as there could be when you're prodded along by an enemy SoldierBot inside a tower controlled by a militaristic super AI. If only he could be at The Drake across town.

"Halt," someone ordered from behind. Block kept

walking, unsure if it was meant for them. G5 didn't stop either because Block hadn't ordered him to.

This time the voice was fierce, urgent, and distinctly female. "Stop where you are, SoldierBot G5148 and unknown robot."

Block halted, ready to turn, when G5 rammed into him, nearly knocking him to the floor. "Stop," he said, hoping the guard wouldn't overhear.

G5 paused but didn't turn. The robot detaining them was unlike any Block had encountered before. It was a Mech—militarized, of course—and twice as wide as a SoldierBot with a chest that looked as heavy as a tank, much like Oxford's. The Bot stood eight feet tall, and her steel gray chrome was flecked with blue crystals. The back of her helmet arced, ending in a long sharp point, and a glowing orange pulse of light gleamed on her dark visor.

She stomped over, her steps vibrating the marble floor. "Why did you not stop on my command?"

G5 was oblivious, and the angry Mech swatted his shoulder like an annoying fly, shoving him backward, where he clattered onto the unyielding floor. The Mech grabbed Block around his neck and pushed him against the lobby wall. "What is this?"

Block assumed the Mech was addressing G5, but of course the SoldierBot didn't answer.

The Mech's head tilted at G5, then scanned Block's face. "What are you?"

"CleanerBot X4J6. My name is Block. I won't hurt you. I can't hurt anyone."

She paused, undoubtedly processing thousands, perhaps millions, of scenarios—she was advanced. She released him, and Block slumped against the wall. G5 approached, awaiting Block's instructions.

The Mech spun and faced G5. "Why are you bringing this inferior model here? It belongs in the scrap piles."

Well, this wasn't going well. Block had hoped to avoid any conversations where G5 might be required to think on his feet—an impossible task given his lack of CPU control.

But G5 followed Block's orders. "I am taking the CleanerBot to command center, level 44."

"Why?"

"Commander Zane wishes to see this one."

Her orange visor beam pulsed, questioning. "For what purpose?"

G5 shrugged, a move that surprised Block. When Oxford had been hacked, he'd been transformed into an automaton, completely devoid of personality. So why was G5 so convincing all of a sudden?

The Mech stared at Block, weaving her orange scanner across his face. What was she doing—analyzing him, or something?

Then she looked back at G5. "As you were. Make it fast though. Commander Zane does not like unnecessary distractions."

"Understood." G5 shoved Block toward the elevator bank—a little too convincingly. The elevator buttons had been ripped out of the wall and replaced by a device the robots preferred. G5 inserted a metal digit into the elevator console and stepped back, waiting beside Block.

Once the elevator descended, four SoldierBots poured out, nodding at G5 before brushing past. The last SoldierBot to emerge poked a finger into Block's chest. "CleanerBot! What a piece of crap. Haven't seen one of these in ages."

His SoldierBot buddy asked, "How many of those did you waste, X-L?"

"At least ten." He stared at G5 through a dark, emotionless visor. "When you're finished, bring this dust machine to me so I can make it eleven." He strode off, joining the others, their jeers floating back as they rounded the corner into the lobby.

Block stepped inside the elevator, relieved to get out of their way. This was the first time he'd ever been around so many SoldierBots at once, and he finagled a bit of code to tune down his threat indicator, otherwise it would have flooded his system and distracted him from the mission.

All he had to do was stay focused—reach the communications hub, sabotage it, and find Wally. He could do it. He had to.

As they ascended in the elevator alone, Block said, "That was a close call with the Mech. You did well."

G5 nodded so imperceptibly that Block assumed his motion sensors were glitching. He couldn't fix that now. "Remember, you need to place this device into command's communications hub." Block retrieved the antenna device that Shane had handed him. Well, technically Shane had handed it to Nova who handed it to him because Shane didn't want to be seen conversing with a lowly CleanerBot.

G5 took it. "Understood."

"And then we find Wally. You need to ask them where the girl is."

G5 jerked his head to one side. "Not understood."

"You need to ask one of the SoldierBots, not the Commander. We need to avoid Commander Zane even though you *said* you are going to see him. Ask any of the SoldierBots where they are keeping the human girl. Do you understand?"

"Understood."

"Oh, and if possible, please protect me from injury."

They were nearing the 44th floor. At any moment the doors would open, and Block wasn't sure what they would be walking into. "Find out the girl's location and take me there. If anyone asks, say it's a classified mission from General Kip."

"Understood."

The elevator door chimed and swooshed open. Block stepped out and faced two lines of SoldierBots, each six units thick.

Their fully automatic rifles all pointed at his chest.

Chapter 23
Reverbatron

Block's threat indicator, though suppressed, surged to its maximum as twelve machine gun barrels stood in his path.

Logic dictated this was his end of service. His parts would begin shutting down systematically, one by one. The moment hung, undisturbed. His split-second processing slowed time to a point where he could think . . . but only for an instant. He had mere fractions of a second left.

There was nothing after termination—only endless black nothingness—an emptiness that even his advanced computing could not fathom.

Please let Wally be okay. Let her live a long life.

Lowering his head, Block steadied himself for his inevitable destruction.

But G5 pushed Block behind his armored body. "What's the meaning of this?"

The first SoldierBot had a blue stripe emblazoned

across her smoky gray visor. "We were alerted to a security breach. Searching for intruders."

Block cowered behind G5, trying to make himself smaller. How was it that he was here, surrounded by nothing but SoldierBots on this impossible mission?

G5 stood his ground, seemingly undeterred by the threat of bullets that might shred his own CPU. "Check the lobby level. There is suspicious activity down there. A Mech guard is glitching and harassing others."

Blue Stripe hesitated, glancing at a SoldierBot across from her, likely confirming and corroborating the intel. "Appreciate the tip. Step aside."

G5 swept his arms behind him, directing Block to stay close as he stepped to the right of the elevator door. The SoldierBots hustled into the elevator and jammed themselves in. Block's hospitality safety programming prompted him to question the elevator's weight limit, but he suppressed the urge to talk.

The doors were closing and G5 surged forward, thrusting his hand inside to stop them. "Where is the human child? I was told to deliver a message to her keepers."

Block's neural circuits buzzed in distress. What was G5 doing? There were twelve deadly SoldierBots that had nearly been out of their way, and G5 was revealing their course. Apparently, the idea of subtlety didn't transfer during a programming hack. It was all Block could do to not run away and hide.

Blue Stripe shook her head. "I don't have that info—"

"Isn't the lab on ten?" asked a SoldierBot who was shoved all the way against the elevator wall.

"Level ten? Yes. That's the place where humans would be," Blue Stripe said, and a few others nodded.

"Understood." G5 let the door close. The elevator dinged pleasantly as it descended.

Alone in the hallway with G5, Block could hardly believe what had happened. "How did you know to ask them? They were sent to kill us."

G5 stared blankly.

Block could practically hear Nova's voice in his feed. Had she been there, she would've said something like, *Get it together, Tin Man.* That reminded him that he hadn't checked in with her. He tapped the small communicator on his chest. He was lucky it hadn't been knocked off when the lobby Mech had grabbed him.

"Nova, are you there?"

Seconds later, her voice buzzed in his feed. "Yes. What's happening in there? You went radio silent on me."

"I can't risk being detected. I'm fine. So far, this is working."

"Have you gotten the antenna inside the comms hub yet?"

"We're working on it." Two SoldierBots rounded the corner and strode down the hallway. Block pressed against the wall and grabbed G5's arm to pull him back too. The SoldierBots passed by without a glance or nod.

"I must go. Will check in soon." Block tapped the mic, cutting Nova off.

The less she knew—the less she worried—the better. Given the sheer number of armed SoldierBots and the possibility of more Mechs like the one downstairs, Block's odds of making it out alive declined with every passing second.

Still, the urge to locate Wally overrode everything—his programming, his threat indicator, even his self-preservation directive.

Block looked at G5. "Install the antenna in the comms hub."

"Understood." G5 spun on his heels and marched down the hall.

Block hurried after him. "I'm your prisoner, remember?" Did he have to spell everything out to the SoldierBot?

G5 hesitated, glancing sideways at him. "Prisoner." His voice went flat as he aimed his gun at Block's chest. Block raised his arms in surrender.

"Protect the prisoner," G5 said.

"Keep your voice down."

Down the hall, the two SoldierBots who had passed by earlier waited at the elevator bank, so Block chose the opposite direction, pacing in front of G5, acting the part of the captive. The hallway traced the edges of the boxy tower. The 44th floor view was stunning, and Block stole glances at nearby rooftops where wild grass and vines had consumed several abandoned penthouse gardens. SoldierBots had no use for plants and vegetables. What a shame. Block had enjoyed harvesting the plants from The Drake's garden. He'd given them to the chef who was always kind and thanked him. The herbs and vegetables were used in many of the dishes that pleased the guests. And pleasing guests pleased Mr. Wallace, and that was all Block had needed back then.

They reached the end of the hallway and veered left, then another turn past a second set of elevator banks. After that, there was nowhere else to go but a broad, open room that was once an office, but all the desks had been stripped away and replaced with machines that lined the walls. Two tall, freestanding units had been placed in the center of the room, and a line of SoldierBots waited to enter them.

The machines sat on a raised platform, and one SoldierBot stepped into the left unit. The doors wrapped shut around it, and the interior lit up with a frantic blue light. Tendrils of electricity surged within and seemed to zap lightning bolts at the SoldierBot. Was it a scanner? Block wanted to ask G_5 but didn't want to blow their cover.

Three waiting SoldierBots stared at them. Block stood out like the ridiculously inferior robot he was. He had to do something quick.

"Get us out of here." But he said it so low, it was barely audible, and it was too late anyway.

The SoldierBot at the end of the line spoke up.

"G5? I met you earlier on the Madison Street patrol. What's new? Who's your prisoner there?"

G5 just nodded.

"Here, take the spot in front of me. I'm in no hurry."

Oh, great. A polite SoldierBot.

The friendly SoldierBot continued, "It would be fun to watch the CleanerBot go inside the Reverbatron."

Polite but still mean. G5 stared.

"Why so quiet? That's not like you. You definitely need a tune up more than I do." The SoldierBot gestured for G5 to take his spot in the line.

G5 stepped forward, accepting the offer, and pulled Block close.

"Excuse me," Block asked quietly. "What does the Reverbatron do, exactly?"

"Cute. It's like your pet," the SoldierBot acquaintance said. He patted Block's head, only his touch was so hard that Block had to fight to stay standing.

"G5, didn't you tell it about the Reverbatron? It's like a facelift for your core processor. It tightens you up, strengthens your programming, and wipes away any kind of stray glitches, or any urge to disobey orders."

Block stared at the dual machines. Another two SoldierBots had gone through and exited the other side, moving the line forward.

Wiping away programming did not sound good. That meant G5 would not be subject to Block's hacking device anymore. Worse, Block couldn't risk his core processor being reprogrammed. That would be a disaster.

"But it's only for SoldierBots, right?"

"I'm not sure if any CleanerBots have ever gone through. I guess we'll see what happens. That ought to be interesting. G5, you've never been this quiet before. You definitely need to be reverberated."

The line advanced another space, so they were only two spots from the machine, and G5 still clutched the disruptor antenna in his hands. What would the Reverbatron do to that piece of equipment?

"Say, I noticed a huge mess in the hallway back there," Block said. "It looked like a SoldierBot had spilled out its microbial cavity."

"So what?" the SoldierBot asked.

Crap. SoldierBots didn't care about bad odor or keeping things clean. What *did* they care about?

"I better go clean it up," Block said.

"What would be the point?"

"Well, G5 said that General Kip is arriving soon. That spill can attract spiders, flies, and—"

"G5, is that true? The General is visiting us? Here?"

"Yes, that's what G5 told me." Block stood next to G5 and grasped for the antenna, grabbing it from G5, hoping no one else noticed a suspicious ten-inch piece of comms equipment.

G5 nodded in agreement, now only one spot away from the Reverbatron. Block had less than a minute to spare before his own programming got wiped out.

"Then get going." The SoldierBot shoved Block toward the hallway. "Clean it up ASAP, you weakling. And if I see one hint of fluid on that carpet, I will personally strip you apart."

So much for the politeness. Block stumbled on his way out of the room and glanced back as G5 stepped inside the Reverbatron.

Block needed to find the comms hub fast. The hacking device buzzed inside his thigh compartment, so he retrieved it. The screen flashed: *Target control severed.*

The Reverbatron had done its work after all. The device updated its status: *Waiting for new target.*

Was it worth all the trouble of hacking a SoldierBot again? They were rather annoying, though G5 had been decent to him.

Where was that comms hub? All he needed to do was get inside and plant the antenna somewhere hidden. Two SoldierBots paced the hall after their turn in the Reverbatron. Block extended his cleaning tube and vacuumed along the side of the wall, hunching his shoulders and making himself as small as possible.

The SoldierBots advanced and paused in front of Block. It was G5 and the SoldierBot from the line.

Trouble.

The SoldierBot slapped Block on the back, hard. "I don't see you cleaning the microbial spill."

"I noticed dust in the corners along the wall." Block glanced at G5, expecting the SoldierBot to turn him in for hacking—or destroy him.

But G5 stared at him with no recognition. "Get to work, CleanerBot." He walked away, but his friend kicked Block in the ankle and said, "Dumb CleanerBot."

They disappeared into the elevators, leaving the hallway clear. Block hurried, still clutching his vacuum cleaner hose and Shane's antenna. Rounding the corner, he spied a room enclosed in tall glass windows and an open door. Inside, equipment hummed from a massive array of elaborate machines, antennas, and other equipment. This had to be the hub.

But there was a problem. A Mech guarded the door, its gun cannons fully armed as it leaned back on its legs, poised for defense. It did not look polite. Not in the least.

Chapter 24
There's more to it than that

Block scrambled to step out of view, but it was too late—the guard Mech had spotted him. The sleek, weaponized machine straightened and surged forward on surprisingly limber hydraulic legs. She didn't bother extending her hands as she ran, which converted into gun barrels. Why bother when she could easily crush Block's head with a single swipe?

"Intruder, identify yourself."

Block waved his vacuum hose. "Greetings. I'm here to clean." He pinged his make and model, opening himself up for inspection by the Mech. His threat indicator buzzed as she poked and prodded at his archives. He exposed a memory of dusting the lobby at The Drake, which seemed to satisfy the Mech.

"What are you doing on this level?"

Block pointed at the room beyond the glass walls. "I was sent because there was a spill inside the hub, and I'm supposed to put this back where it belongs." He held out the small antenna. "I was assigned to clean this part." He knew this was a risky move. The Mech could figure out that it was sabotage, destroy the device—and Block's CPU—in seconds. But Block had one thing going for him. Every SoldierBot and Mech so far had underestimated him. They expected him to be weak and meant for nothing beyond cleaning.

"Who sent you?"

Crap. That was the one question Block was hoping wouldn't get asked. With the hacking black box still hidden in his thigh, should he try to take control of the Mech guard?

"Was it BVon?" she asked. "I can't stand him. Always second-guessing me and challenging my authority because he rolled off the line twenty minutes before me." She stared at Block, her visor scanning him with an undulating gold-yellow pulse.

Block nodded. "Yes. BVon."

"I thought so. Fine. Go and be quick. I don't want you up here for long. Don't make me come and find you."

"I won't." Block extended his hose and vacuum brushes as he entered the comms hub. The strange computing units buzzed and hummed around him. He suspected the antenna would disrupt whatever machinery was nearby. He didn't know the specifics but assumed it would interfere with the SoldierBots' surveillance methods throughout the city. The broken signals would help Shane's forces move about and perhaps infiltrate the tower. Block was supposed to inform Nova as soon as the job was completed, to alert the human troops who were standing by, ready to attack. She would probably already be furious at him for not reporting his status, but he'd have to explain how dangerous this had been.

Then again, he was counting on *not* seeing her ever again. It would be the best thing for Wally—so humans wouldn't keep her away from Block again. A weird twitching spun in his core processor when he calculated scenarios, especially ones where Nova was absent.

No time to process though, he needed to hurry and get to the lab on floor ten before Shane's troops attacked.

A SoldierBot stood inside the room, its helmet linked to a machine along the wall. Block didn't need more trouble and avoided that corner, instead vacuuming bits of dust along the bright white floor. The room was clean somehow since it only contained equipment. Usually SoldierBots were so sloppy, but they'd been careful in the hub. He scanned the wall units with their blinking lights and intimidating interfaces, looking for an empty spot where the antenna could be fixed, yet hidden. Pretending to inspect the digital displays for dust, Block blasted compressed air through the cracks and crevices. The guard Mech rotated her broad head, watching Block from outside the room.

He was running out of time.

Block paused before a machine that displayed a screen with GPS coordinates. Large red dots on the screen flickered—glowing—and Block captured the image and saved it to his memory archives. He recognized it was a map of the city with different locations, but he didn't know what the flashing spots meant. He could decipher it later.

At hip-level, he opened a storage tray in the computer unit which had just enough room to stand the antenna up next to a bunch of green and blue wires. It would have to do. He sprayed a little adhesive, fixed it in place, and closed the drawer. Job done.

He passed the Mech on his way out. She said, "Tell BVon, he's an ass."

"Will do."

He headed toward the elevator and pressed the down button as three SoldierBots turned the corner and strode his way. A nearby door led to a stairwell, so he pushed beyond its doors and started down. Traveling the length from level forty-four to ten was a long, long way. but the elevators were risky. He didn't want to be caught, yet there was a highly probably chance the stairwells were guarded too. Masquerading as the tower CleanerBot had been working out decently so far. Would it keep working?

He made it down five floors before running into a guard. Swishing his vacuum hose, trying desperately to appear busy, he crossed the platform to the next level where a SoldierBot sat in the stairwell. A rifle lay stretched across its lap, and the Bot sat with its back against the wall.

Block sent a friendly ping—the kind of courteous,

self-deprecating ping that a lowly hospitality robot sent to a military model. The guard replied and Block knew him.

G5 raised his hand. "Stop," he said over the blare of the vacuum.

Block switched the suction off. This was trouble. Of all the hundreds—thousands?—of robots he could have run into, it had to be the one he'd hijacked.

G5 stared at him. "What did you do to me?"

Threat sensors blaring in his feed, Block hesitated.

G5 shook his head like a human with water in the ear. "My sensors register that something is different."

Was this a side effect from hacking? Did G5 remember? Nothing had gone wrong with Oxford, but that had been a different device.

"I don't understand," Block said. "Did I do something wrong? I'm just a CleanerBot."

"Of course, you are. My sensors are buzzing, telling me I know you from somewhere, but I can't access any memory files to prove it." G5 thumped his visor with his fist. "Were you standing in line at the Reverbatron earlier?"

"I was there briefly. I was attempting to locate a spill that I was assigned to clean."

"Then that explains it."

Block began to shuffle along, hoping to pass by and continue downstairs.

He'd managed two steps when G5 said, "No. There's more to it than that." He stood. "I saw you outside the tower too. You're up to something."

"You must have me confused with someone else." Block took one more step down, then another, keeping his gaze down on the concrete steps.

"You're searching for a human girl."

That froze Block in mid step.

"And I have no freaking clue why, but I want to help you. Will you look at me, CleanerBot?"

Block swiveled his head, fearful to defy the SoldierBot. What would happen when G_5 realized the full extent of Block's deception?

"We need to go to the lab on level ten," G_5 said.

This was completely unexpected and went against all logic. Oxford had never reported any long-term side effects from the hacking device, but then again, he was a lot stronger than a SoldierBot.

Had Block stumbled upon some kind of AI mind-control device? He stood there, watching G_5, unsure how to proceed.

"Well, start moving," G_5 said. "My electrodes aren't getting any younger standing here. I'll help you get to floor ten and find the human you're looking for."

"I don't understand why you're helping me."

"I have no idea either. But I'm compelled to do so. Something in my wiring."

"Please don't tell anyone. If the others found out I'm searching for a human—"

"I'm not an idiot. Yes, I understand that. Let's go."

Block descended the stairs to the next level, G_5 trailing him, and tapped the comm.

"What's happening?" Nova asked. Her voice had a weird, shaky tremor.

"It's been tricky in here."

"You can't go radio silent on me. You're leaving us blind out here." The comm clicked off as she muted her end. Shane was probably there. Or Kalin or Pete, someone she didn't want Block to hear.

"I'm not exactly alone in this tower," he said. "Multiple intimidating Bots have questioned me."

"Did you plant the antenna?" Click, then silence.

That was all she cared about. Typical. Wanting her way, but he needed to stall. If Shane's troops attacked before he'd escaped with Wally, his hopes of getting her out safely were out the window.

"Block? You there?"

"Please repeat," Block said, though he'd heard her perfectly.

G_5 said, "Hurry up and lower your voice output."

"I'm trying." Block hadn't muted himself. Oops.

"Who are you talking to?" Nova asked.

"The SoldierBot. It got confused."

"Did you plant the antenna or not?"

Block's logic processor spun, churning out 267 scenarios in a few milliseconds. Answering no meant a 68 percent probability of escaping with Wally. Saying yes ended with an 89.6 percent chance of getting captured or struck down by SoldierBots or humans.

"No. I'm in view of the comms hub, but I haven't figured out how to get inside yet."

"Oh, hell." She paused on her end, probably arguing with Shane about what to do.

"We're out of time," she said. "Can you plant the antenna where you are now? If you're in view of the room . . . even on the same floor, it's close enough."

Drats. He'd passed level thirteen. He was so close to the lab, he just needed ten more minutes.

Lying to Nova made his sensors whir. Why couldn't he have been programmed with a tiny bit more deviousness?

"I'll plant the antenna, but I need more time to get rid of the guard in the hallway."

"We have eyes on the 44th floor. A sniper's in place at the building across from you. Let us know who to take out. Is it the big robot that's standing in front of the hub?"

What? How did they possibly have a sniper? Could they really take down a Mech? But the guard hadn't hurt him—she didn't deserve that.

"Where are you located? The sniper doesn't see you," Nova said.

Block halted on the stairwell platform just outside the door onto level ten. "Hold your fire."

"Why? We're out of time. The longer we wait, the more chance this mission will fail."

"I've almost managed to reach a safe spot where I can plant the antenna. You don't have to fire and reveal your sniper's position. If you shoot, drones and Soldier-Bots will descend within a minute."

"Shane says we can't wait anymore. Leave the antenna and get out of there."

"But I haven't gotten Wally yet!"

"Sorry . . . We have to start now. I don't have a choi—"

Click. He tapped the comm again, hoping to restore the connection, but there was only static. Nova's comms had been shut off.

Shane was going to ruin everything.

Chapter 25
That's what I was built for

"We must hurry." The sign on the tenth-floor security door read: *Restricted Access*. Block tested the handle anyway and found it locked. "Can you open it?"

G5 placed a chrome hand on the ID scanner, and it flashed red, then: *Entry Denied*. "I don't have the right permission level."

Great. Not even a SoldierBot could get onto the lab floor.

"How do we get in? We must access this door." Block could not give up this close to Wally.

G5 smashed his fist into the ID scanner, shattering the display face and sending glass shards and circuit bits clattering to the floor.

Block edged away. "That's not going to do any good."

But G5 ignored him and slammed his body into the door so that a violent clattering of metal screeching against metal arose. The door didn't budge, but it dented. G5 rammed it again, and this time his arm and shoulder were bent in—crushed. His attempts were working—the door seemed to be caving in.

"You're hurting yourself," Block said.

"You must get through, and there's little time." G5 rammed once more, this time breaching the door. His tackle collapsed the steel barrier, and he landed on the hallway floor, skidding to a stop after a four-foot slide.

Block followed him into the lab area. G5's left arm hung by two cables attached to his shoulder's hydraulic joint. Block stared at it, assessing how badly damaged the robot was.

"It's no matter. Go find your human. I'll be right behind."

The tower's security alarm blared suddenly, emitting a shrill beep loud enough to be heard by every Bot in the vicinity. He hoped Wally wasn't exposed for too long; it could damage her hearing. Block raced through the hall, ignoring a robot about his size who called out from inside a room.

"Wally! Where are you?" Block wished he had some way to communicate with her. Before they parted, she'd started saying one or two words—she knew his name. "Wally, wherever you are, yell something!"

He sprinted through the hallway, scanning inside each room. Two rooms were filled with old office equipment. Another had counters piled high with lab equipment: tubes, vials, bottles, and strange equipment that looked like 3D printers. He passed a room that contained a child-sized tub surrounded by hospital equipment. The floor appeared empty of any threatening robots.

Block kept running, his steel feet clanking against the hard tile. Behind him, the lab robot followed and tried to speak. G5 pushed it against the wall in a choke hold, but by then, Block had almost reached the end of the hall.

Where was Wally?

His logic processor said there should be more SoldierBots, maybe even a Mech, especially after all the trouble Mach X had gone through to secure Wally in the first place. Was everyone distracted by the alarms? Were Shane's troops causing a big disturbance outside? If so, the SoldierBots would be activating and descending in elevators and filing downstairs to fend off the attack.

"Wally!" He reached the end of the hall and found a room with glass walls that looked in on three lines of cribs, all of them meant for children who were Wally's size.

She had to be here.

He pressed against the door leading in, expecting it to be locked, but it gave way, and he burst through. "Wally, where are you?" The sides of the cribs were high enough that he couldn't see into all of them. He searched the first three—empty. Rumpled white sheets. The next row was empty, too, and the next.

Nine cribs and not a single human child inside them.

He scanned the room's interior for any kind of clue. Scattered old equipment littered the floor, and along the walls only empty spots stood. It didn't take the dust-sensing capabilities of a CleanerBot to notice that large, rectangular indentations marred the floor and several spots where objects had rested were void of dirt.

Had the spots been occupied by machines that monitored the children, ones like the Incubator unit he'd met when he found Wally?

Block raced back into the hallway in front of a window that faced outside. At street level, three rows of SoldierBots formed barricades. It would be nearly impossible to make it out undetected.

G5's boots clanked down the hallway toward him, and he dragged the lab robot by one arm. Its model was similar to a FactoryBot, its frame as weak as a Cleaner-Bot. The machine was no threat, even Block knew that.

G5 tossed the robot forward, sending him crashing into a heap at Block's feet. "This one will have answers for you."

The lab robot stared up at Block and raised its hands in surrender. "Please don't hurt me. I was only doing what they told me."

Block stared down at the weaker being. "Where's the child? The one named Wally. Is she on a different floor?"

"Which child? They were all the same to me."

More than one?

"The cribs were full. There were other lab robots and SoldierBots, but they moved everything out suddenly last night. They made me stay behind. I don't know why."

Block's sensors buzzed; his processor churned. "Where did they go?"

"They loaded everything onto a transport jet on the roof. One of them said they were headed for New York City, to Mach X's headquarters."

Block sank to his knees, lowered his hands, and hung his head. The entire journey, risking everything, and he'd just missed Wally.

"Where in New York City?" G5 asked.

"You think they'd tell me?"

G5 kicked the robot in the side and thrust a fist in his face. "If you're lying to us—"

"I promise. It's the truth." Then the lab bot looked at Block. "They didn't tell me, of course, but I overheard rumors that Mach X's headquarters are located near the Empire State building."

"What were they doing to the children here?" Block asked. "What did they do to the girl that recently arrived?"

The lab Bot's eyes lit up with a blue glow. "You must be the robot the SoldierBots were talking about—the one that was protecting her. They made you sound like a powerful and clever bot who had hidden her and outsmarted Mach X, but I never would've guessed it was you, now that I see you. You're just a CleanerBot."

G5 kicked him again. Hard.

"Hey! I'm cooperating."

"Answer Block's question."

"The SoldierBots and the NannyBot had the children here, and they were studying them. I took samples—blood, hair, mucus, and saliva. That's what I was built for. I'm a medical HelperBot, but without humans around, I've been out of work. I was living in the tunnels underneath the city with a lot of other useless bots—hospitality, FactoryBots, others. Anyway, a bunch of SoldierBots came in and cleaned out the tunnels one day. Turns out they were picking up hospital types like me. They brought me here and made me look after this bunch of children."

"There was a NannyBot here?" Block asked.

"Yes. One I'd never encountered before. A new, advanced model. It didn't say a lot, but everyone—even the SoldierBots—stayed out of its way."

"Why?"

"Have you ever seen a NannyBot equipped with attack drones and an armor-piercing gun cannon?"

"No." Block had never heard of armed NannyBots. Was this the same model that Cybel had mentioned leading the attack on the desert mine? His threat indicator flashed—Wally was being minded by a killer NannyBot. This was not computing at all.

"How many children were here?" Block asked.

"Nine clones total. There's a boy kind and a girl kind, genetically identical. They were making more, or at least, they were about to before they decided to haul out of here."

"They what? How could they possibly make more children here?"

"I could hardly believe it myself," the HelperBot said. "But that's what X has been doing. It figured out a way to clone humans and has been growing them, monitoring them. I know that they're given some kind of implants. Probably a chip that tracks them."

"It's more than that," Block said.

"How so?"

"The girl I protected—Wally—she has a neural implant that allows X to observe everything she does."

"That's extreme. Are the implants in all of the kids?"

"I don't know."

Something buzzed and chirped, and G5 raised his right hand to his head, listening. "I'm getting orders to report to ground level and defend the tower. Human rebels are attacking."

"Yes, I know," Block said.

G5 looked through the window. "The situation outside is dangerous. You won't make it out."

"There's no point anyway. I've lost Wally."

"What are you talking about?" G5 asked. "Thanks to this lab rat, you know exactly where she is. You have to get to New York City."

"But that will take days, possibly weeks, and I'm just a CleanerBot. How could I possibly get inside Mach X's headquarters?"

"I don't know." G5 made a funny silhouette against the window with his damaged arm hanging awkwardly at his side. He hoisted his rifle up on the intact shoulder. "You'll have to figure it out on the way there."

"Yeah," the HelperBot said. "There were at least nine children here, and there might be more in New York City. You can find a way in. You got inside here, didn't you?"

Block couldn't believe he was getting a pep talk from a SoldierBot and a HelperBot, but life had been unexpected and strange ever since the Uprising. They were right. He couldn't give up. Not now, after all this time—Wally was still in trouble.

Block looked at the two robots. "How do I get out of here?"

"I see no way to get past the battle taking place on the streets surrounding the tower," G5 said.

"What about the roof?"

"There's a landing pad for a jet, but it's heavily guarded. No way out but down."

Block could signal Nova, warn her that he was coming out. But how would that work when he couldn't get past the SoldierBots defending the tower?

The HelperBot said, "I know a way out."

G5 stomped. "Don't waste our time. How would you know about this tower?"

"I know what's underneath the tower," he said. "I used to live in the city *underneath* the city."

Chapter 26
Sapient scum

G5's boots stomped against the tenth-floor corridor tiles as he pushed Block and the HelperBot in a wheeled cart. The cart's interior barely fit the two robots, and Block had to lay doubled over, leaning on top of the other Bot's contorted metal parts.

"Do you have a name?" Block asked.

"920-TL."

"That's hard to say. How about a nickname?"

"The SoldierBots called me Lab Rat."

"That's mean," Block said. "I won't call you that. What's your favorite lab tool?"

"My favorite tool? No idea. I liked caring for the children and feeding them."

"Then, how about we call you Spoon?"

"Spoon? I like that."

G5 kicked the cart in warning as the elevator dinged, followed by a rush of warm, trapped air as the doors swooshed open. Block and Spoon were hidden behind a sheet that G5 had wrapped over and around the cart's sides. Stray pieces of lab equipment lay scattered on top, and it looked as though G5 was like any dutiful SoldierBot moving spare parts to a new location.

Block could hardly believe the SoldierBot was still helping him, that G5 had adopted his mission. He would have to tell Maxwell about this strange side effect—if that's what it was—from the hacking device. Block carried the black box in his storage compartment, knowing Maxwell would want to study it in earnest.

The cart's clunky wheels rumbled over the elevator's entry gap as G5 pushed it inside the elevator, jarring Block and Spoon. They were not alone. Though his comm was cloaked, Block picked up the energy signatures of other AI nearby.

"What's that?" a voice asked.

"Equipment from the lab on ten," G5 said. "I was ordered to bring it down to the basement."

"That looks like junk to me. Ditch it and come with us. We're about to pick off a bunch of humans. Sapient scum."

"There's nothing I would like better, but I have my orders. I'll join you as soon as I drop this off in the basement."

"Suit yourself." The elevator came to a stop, and what sounded like ten or more pairs of boots echoed as they filed out. The cart stayed still—Block acutely aware of all vibrations inside the dark hiding spot—and a chime sounded as the elevator door shut. Block's motion sensors registered the rapid descent to the basement level.

The door had just opened when Nova signaled Block. He tapped the comm mic.

"Block, come in," she said into his feed.

"Here," he said, only his voice was so low, he couldn't be sure the microphone would even register it. Block wasn't completely sure they were safe. It was up to G5 to steer them toward the underground pedway that Spoon had described. The HelperBot had sheltered in the network of underground tunnels and passageways that connected major Chicago buildings and transportation centers in the city's financial district. The system offered residents an escape from harsh winter days and relief from the throngs of tourists that descended on the city during the warm months.

That was before the Uprising. Now, the underground was abandoned, left to robot escapees, scavengers, and occasional SoldierBot raids. For Block's crew—it was the perfect place in which to disappear.

"Don't know why, but the SoldierBots hate it down here," Spoon said as G5 peeled back the sheet once they were another building's length away from the old Sears Tower.

"Because it's a place for bottom feeders like you," G5 said. "SoldierBots don't need to creep around in the darkness. We rule the city."

"There you go. An insight into a SoldierBot's psyche."

Block ignored their banter and paced a few feet

away for privacy. "Nova, I can talk now." Part of him didn't want to tell her he'd failed his mission.

"Where are you?"

"I'm out of the tower. We managed to get out safely and into the tunnels underground."

"You got her!" Her voice sounded lighter. *"Is she okay?"*

"No. Wally wasn't in the tower."

"What? Where... How did you—"

"Two robots helped me get out safely. She wasn't in the tower, but I have an idea where she is."

"Crap. I'm so sorry. Well, that's good you know where she is. We'll find her. Also, I'm glad you're out safely. I need to come get you."

"What about the battle?"

"I'll explain later. Give me your GPS coordinates, and I'll come find you."

"But where are Shane and the others?"

"They're still charging the tower's defenses. I've separated for now to come help you. You planting the antenna helped a lot. It knocked out the SoldierBots' comms, and Shane's people are hitting them in strategic spots all over the city."

Block hesitated. He'd failed to find Wally, yet he'd managed to succeed at creating more mass destruction—against his own kind, no less.

"What do you want with me?"

Her breathing was faster—barely perceptible to his auditory sensors. "Shane wants me to escort you back to O'Hare. We'll have troops and a vehicle this time. No more walking and being shot at."

Block had assumed he would make the return journey on his own now that Nova was reunited with Shane and other humans. It only seemed natural that she would stay there and fight for their cause.

Still, he wasn't exactly looking forward to dodging snipers or human scavengers along the train tracks. Riding in a vehicle and being protected by troops was appealing.

"If you're driving with Kalin and Pete, you can forget it."

"They aren't coming," she said. "I made sure of it."

Block glanced at G5 and Spoon. He didn't know what they wanted to do next, and he still had no idea why the SoldierBot hadn't shot him yet. One thing he did know—being around Nova with other robots had been disastrous.

He would have to cut them loose.

He gave Nova the coordinates, then returned to where the SoldierBot and HelperBot were standing.

"Who were you talking to?" G5 asked.

"Someone's coming for me. I'm leaving soon. You can't come with me. Either of you."

Spoon's head swiveled, checking out the empty tunnel basement. A sign on the wall pointed an arrow to an old department store that had once been a tourist destination but had probably been cleared out by looters.

"Fine with me," Spoon said. "I'll go back to living

the life I had before, rummaging in old stores, dodging scavengers, and staying away from SoldierBots."

Block studied the smaller robot. "I'm sorry."

"It wasn't so bad. I didn't like working for Mach X, but I did enjoy the kids."

"Why can't we come with you?" G5 asked. "I can't go back to the tower. Something isn't right with my programming. I still don't know what you did to me."

"My friend is human, and she's with the rebels. I don't want either of you hurt."

"Who will protect you?" G5 asked.

"She won't hurt me. I'm her . . ." Was *friend* the right word? Block thought so but wasn't entirely sure because Nova didn't always act like his friend. Often, she acted in her own self-interest. Yet she'd helped him get to the tower to find Wally, and she was coming back for him.

Was it possible she was changing in a good way, becoming someone Block could trust?

"If human soldiers are coming for you," G5 argued, "you can't trust them. I could protect you."

"They don't trust robots they don't know—especially SoldierBots. They know me. I'm harmless."

"So am I," Spoon said. "Harmless."

"I could leave my rifle or hand it over to them," G5 said. "You shouldn't go alone."

"I'm joining up with my AI friends out at the airport. They have weapons, and they're waiting for me."

"O'Hare? That's a long way out," G5 said.

"Nova—the woman—is coming to take me there."

"Let me get this straight," G5 said. "Human rebel soldiers are coming to take you to your *armed* robot friends at O'Hare? Does that sound safe to you, Spoon?"

"Sounds sketchy to me."

"Nova is someone I've known a long time. I traveled with her, and she owes me. She's offered to bring me back to O'Hare where I started, and I'm taking her up on it because there are snipers along the route. They shot at Nova and me before."

That quieted them.

"I really appreciate the help both of you gave me," Block said. "I couldn't have done this without you two, especially you, G5."

His logic module reminded him that he'd changed G5's programming—possibly forever. "There's something you should know. I used a black box hacking device to commandeer you and get inside the tower."

G5 pointed at his chest. "You hacked into *me*?"

"Yes. You happened to be in my way, and I chose you. That's why your programming has been altered."

"Now the scenario makes more sense. How do I go back to the way I was?"

"I don't know. Try the Reverbatron?"

"I already went through that. It didn't help."

"What will they do if they catch you?" Spoon asked.

"Probably scrap me. Wipe out my core and start over."

"I've never seen a SoldierBot living in the tunnels. You'll be a target, that's for certain," Spoon said.

Block processed dozens of scenarios—Spoon and G5 wandering through abandoned stores of junk, hiding from scavengers, and eventually being caught by patrolling SoldierBots. It was not a life he wished on anyone.

But he couldn't waste any more time in finding Wally.

"I have to go now." Block turned and hurried away. He needed to find the Washington Street station, where Nova had said to wait.

Something twitched in his circuitry. He tried to shove it away, like a bad kernel of code. But the intrusive sequence lingered.

Something deep in his programming forced him to consider—

he'd abandoned Vacuubot once, and that had proven to be a mistake.

Treading through the dark passage, night vision engaged, Block dodged mounds of garbage on the floor. He did his best to ignore them, reminding himself that Nova was on her way. As he fought the urge to clean, he glanced back at G5 and Spoon who huddled together.

He was far enough away, and his plan to get rid of them had worked. It had been easy, in fact. All he'd had to do was tell them no.

Only something didn't sit right.

He was abandoning someone again. *But they're perfectly capable.*

He turned one last time and waved goodbye. G5's battered arm hung from his side as he and Spoon watched Block leave.

They're perfectly...

Block turned back.

Chapter 27
Awaiting instructions

Block lingered in the deep stairwell that led from the Washington Street sidewalk down into the train tunnel entrance. This was where Nova had said she would retrieve him. After a minute, he poked his head up, looking for her.

In the distance came the crack of gunfire echoing among the abandoned, rotting office buildings. Three drones buzzed overhead, and he ducked into the stairwell, taking cover, but they kept on going, heading somewhere fast.

Another minute passed before a heavy vehicle rumbled down the street—a beaten, shot-up gray truck that had a body like a tank with wheels the size of Oxford's fists. Block was about to retreat into the stairwell, uncertain whether it was an enemy vehicle, when a side door opened and Nova jumped out onto the cracked street. She scanned up and down the avenue, then tiptoed to the stairwell. "Hey, you down there?"

Block poked his head up. "Here I am." He raised his arms to be sure she knew he was unarmed. A ponytailed soldier he didn't recognize leaned over the side of the truck and aimed a rifle at the nearby buildings, scanning for threats.

On spotting Block, Nova's eyebrows raised and the lines around her mouth softened. "What are you waiting for? Let's go."

He climbed another step, still partially hidden in the stairwell. "I have two robots with me, and I'd like to bring them along. If you can't take all of us, I guess we'll go on our own."

Nova stiffened like she suddenly had a pain in her neck. "What do you mean two robots? What kind of robots? You didn't tell me!"

Block ventured onto the sidewalk and gestured for G5 and Spoon to follow him. "One is a medical HelperBot which could be useful to your troops, and the other, well . . ."

"Holy crap." Nova drew the Glock on her hip and aimed at the SoldierBot.

"G5 is unarmed," Block said.

Nova glanced behind her at the truck. "Hold your fire." She raised her hand at the woman soldier, then frowned at Block. "You're telling me you want to bring a SoldierBot with us to O'Hare?"

"I know it seems strange, and by all accounts it should be impossible, but I hacked into G5"—Block jerked a steel thumb at the SoldierBot—"with your device and changed his programming. He helped me escape, and now he doesn't have anywhere to go."

"You're absolutely flapping nuts if you think—"

Something exploded down the street, and glass panes from a looted retail shop shattered. Nova flinched, her shoulders hunching. "We're out of time. No way in hell is Shane going to be on board with this. We're shredding SoldierBots, in case you haven't noticed."

G5's left arm swung when he twisted his torso.

"He's injured, not at full strength. Shane won't be so scared. I won't abandon them," Block said. "We'll travel on our own if we have to."

The female soldier whistled sharply. "Nova, get in! There's a line of SoldierBots advancing. The drones will be here any second."

Nova gritted her teeth at Block. "I hate you right now."

Block stood his ground. "We'll be fine on our own." But his scenario processor declared they had a 32.6 percent survival chance if he and his new robot friends trekked to O'Hare on their own.

Nova cursed and glanced at the armored truck. "I have room for you and the smaller one. The SoldierBot's going to have to ride on the back."

Block looked at G5. "Can you do that?"

"Yes. I'll hold on."

Spoon cowered behind Block, so he grabbed the HelperBot's arm and nudged him toward the truck. "Go ahead. Get in."

Spoon's visor lit up in concern. "But they're armed humans. Are you sure?"

"I know Nova. She won't hurt us." Block hoped he sounded reassuring. Nova wouldn't hurt him. She wouldn't bring physical harm on them unless G5 attacked her. He couldn't say the same about the other soldiers though and hoped they would listen to Nova's orders.

"I'll be right behind you," Block said as Spoon climbed in.

Another explosion rocked the closest tower, and smoke poured out of the stairwell where Block and the others had been only minutes before.

"Come on!" Nova climbed inside and held out her hand for Block.

G5 approached the truck's rear and leaped onto the low bumper, wrapping his fist around a handle on the truck's roof.

"You sure you'll be okay up there?" Block asked.

"I can handle it. Go on, get in."

Block grabbed Nova's fist and slid onto the bench seat next to Spoon. Behind them sat the soldier who had leaned out the window to cover the street. Her auburn hair was tied back in a ponytail.

In the front, a woman wearing a black T-shirt and cap revved the engine and made a wide U-turn, accelerating down Washington. "Why the hell is that SoldierBot on the back bumper?"

"I know it seems crazy," Nova said. "The

SoldierBot is unarmed, and I kept it outside for a reason."

"Will G5 be safe out there?" Block asked.

"Depends on who shoots at it, or if I can knock it off first." The driver veered suddenly, though there were no obstacles on the road.

"Enough, Lena," Nova said. "I'm in charge here. The SoldierBot will be fine—as long as it stays outside. Block, you know as well as I do that thing's armor can withstand bullets. Are you positive it's on your side? How do you know it's not spying on you? That this isn't some trick?"

"I hacked into it and changed it somehow. I can't explain why it happened that way, but yes, I trust G5."

"Block speaks the truth," Spoon said.

Nova glared at him. "And what exactly are you?"

"My name is TL . . . Never mind. Call me Spoon. I'm a medical HelperBot."

"Well, now I've seen everything."

"Spoon was forced to work for Mach X and doesn't want to anymore," Block said. "He took care of Wally and other children."

Nova's eyes widened. "There were other children there?"

"Nine of them," Spoon said. "All clones—"

"Nobody asked for that information," Block said, cutting Spoon off, hoping he would catch the hint. He didn't trust the two women soldiers and questioned whether he could trust Nova.

"What happened to Wally? Where's she now?" Nova asked.

"New York City," Spoon said.

Block would have preferred not to tell her that right now. He would have to talk to Spoon about divulging information without Block's permission.

"They took her to New York?" Nova said. "To Mach X?"

The driver glanced back in the rearview mirror. "Where we'll be headed soon enough."

Nova flinched, and if Block had been a less sophisticated model, he might have missed it entirely.

"You're going to New York?" Block asked. This was unexpected.

"It's part of Shane's plan."

"His plan for what?"

She didn't answer right away, which meant she was either thinking up a lie or framing how to explain something complicated to him—something she assumed a robot wouldn't understand. It was usually one of those two things when humans didn't answer right away.

"Shane wants to defeat X on its home turf."

"You never told me this before," Block said.

Her pupils dilated; he recognized her agitation. How long had she known Shane's plans and not confided in Block?

At the Chicago River, they crossed a bridge with high, rusty arches. Slabs of asphalt in the road had cracked, and jagged pieces littered the street, but the truck's hefty tires rumbled over them as if they were pebbles.

"Are we taking the highway?" Block asked. "It's filled with abandoned vehicles."

"We'll be traveling the side streets next to the highway," the driver said.

"I mapped out a route before we left," Nova said. "Don't worry. We'll get you there safe." But her jaw was tight as she picked at the corners of her fingernails, a habit Block recognized. He'd witnessed her obsessive nail digging before when they'd gotten close to Colorado, and again when Mach X's forces were going to attack Hemlock. Her habit was predictable.

Something was definitely off. Was she planning to trick him? Maybe Vacuubot had been right not to trust her.

"Nova, why don't you let us off at one of the old train stations close to O'Hare. We can make our way from there."

"Why? We can take you the whole way."

"I'd rather not walk in the open," Spoon said.

Block pinged Spoon privately, *Quiet! You're not helping.*

Sorry? Spoon replied. *What did I do wrong?*

Never mind.

Lena, the driver, had a comm earbud from which faint, tinny vibrations emitted—someone was talking to her. Her eyes flicked to the rearview mirror, stopping on Nova's distracted face as she stared out the window at the desolate highway.

"This is the area where the sniper shot at us." She pointed. "See? Over there by the tall evergreens."

"Let's see them shoot at us now," the woman in the back seat said. She grabbed onto a periscope that folded down from the truck's ceiling. The roof of the vehicle thrummed as she unleashed gunfire on the trees and abandoned row houses that lined the side of the highway.

"But you don't know who's there," Block said.

Nova bit her lip but let the woman continue a few beats. "That's enough, Gail. You showed them what was up." But there was no excitement in her voice as her shoulders slumped.

"Damn straight." Gail leaned back in her chair, releasing the gun controls.

Block swiveled his head to check on G5, still perched on the truck's rear exterior. *Are you okay?*

Yes. Who were they shooting at? Why?

They were retaliating at whoever shot at me before.

Block turned back and picked up on the chatter in Lena's earpiece. Though he couldn't make out the words, he knew whoever was talking was excited—they were practically yelling. Lena glanced back and locked eyes with Gail, then nodded slightly. Whatever the two were communicating, Nova seemed left out.

Block wondered why Shane wanted Nova to escort him to the airport so badly. It wasn't like Shane to care one iota about Block's welfare.

Lena veered off the side road and barreled onto the highway for a stretch before exiting onto the ramp that led to O'Hare. At the top of the overpass, a barrier of cars had been formed, blocking access to the road beyond. A hunched-over figure loomed on top of a car —someone guarding the ramp?

Block's vision zoomed in, and his threat indicator surged. Beside him, Nova's breath caught in her throat. A SoldierBot had been bolted onto the car with long iron rods that made it appear to stand on the hood. Painted on the windshield in bold, red letters was: *Kill All Robots*.

Lena rammed the truck through the weakest side of the barricade, crushing past an old Volkswagen sedan like it was a child's toy. She floored the accelerator as they traveled the open road that led to the airport.

Now that he was in range, Block pinged Oxford, hoping his comm channel was open. *On our way.*

Block, glad to hear from you, Oxford replied.

I'm with Nova and two human soldiers. Also, a SoldierBot—he's friendly! And a HelperBot. Do not fire on us. We're in a tank truck.

Got it, Oxford replied. *I won't fire. Glad you warned me.*

Nova's gaze fixed on him. How did she know his quirks so well? "What are you doing?"

"Giving Oxford a heads up that we're coming," Block said.

"Who's Oxford?" Lena asked, frowning.

"The Mech," Nova said, and Lena jammed on the brakes, coming to a grinding halt.

"Why are you stopping?" Nova asked. The airport

arrivals lane loomed another two hundred feet away. "I didn't tell you to stop."

"Awaiting instructions," Lena said.

"I gave you instructions to keep going." Nova drummed her fingers against the barrel of her rifle. "Get us to the airport—now."

In the backseat, Gail pressed her gun barrel against the back of Nova's neck. "You're not in charge."

Chapter 28
These robots do what they want

Four identical armored trucks careened through the highway ramp barricade and accelerated toward them. A dozen or more drones descended from the sky, circling and landing.

Oxford pinged Block, *what's happening out there?*

I'm not sure yet. It's bad.

Inside the cabin, Lena twisted in her seat and grimaced at Nova. "Hand over your rifle."

"Whatever is happening right now," Nova said. "Don't do it. If Shane finds out what you're doing, he'll—"

Lena scoffed. "If Shane finds out? Who do you think ordered us to do this?"

"But he—" Nova bit back her words.

The side door flipped open, and Kalin stood there smirking with her blond hair whipping in the breeze. Pete lurked behind her, having already pinned G5 on the ground with a rifle jammed against his visor.

"Well." Kalin chuckled. "Making more robots friends, are you?" She pursed her lips at Nova. "When will you learn?"

"Where is he?" Nova flushed a shade of crimson, and Block had never seen her throw a more severe death stare.

"You really think Shane has time for this? You're not important enough to him anymore." Her grin turned sour. "Get out." She yanked Nova out of the truck, causing her to stumble and land on her knees.

Oxford pinged. *Block, we're on the tarmac. Can you get to us?*

Not likely.

Maxwell repaired a jet, and we're about to take off.

Nova grunted, and Block's processor churned at high speed. His readings showed her heartbeat pumping like a bee on steroids, while her adrenaline levels soared.

Hold, please. Block didn't want to be rude to Oxford, but too much was happening, what with his friends all having guns jammed in their faces.

"Watch that one," Kalin said to Pete who still trained his rifle on G5.

"When can I waste it?" Pete asked. "I'll string it up next to the Scrapper that was bolted to that car back there on the road."

Kalin grunted. "We need them all intact for the moment."

"Get out, you waste of steel." Kalin shoved her handgun in Spoon's face and pulled the scrawny

HelperBot outside where it bounced against Nova's shoulder, then kneeled beside her.

"Sorry," Spoon said to Nova.

Block knew his turn was next, and he didn't want to be ejected violently like the others. What if he sustained damage? He slid across the bench seat, raising his hands in what he hoped looked like surrender.

But Kalin grabbed him by the shoulder and tossed him down onto the hard asphalt anyway.

"Nice work, ladies." Kalin nodded to Gail and Lena.

"Shane would never go for this," Nova said. "She's lying to you." She tapped a button on her belt and unleashed a cry for help. "Shane, it's Nova. Kalin and Pete have attacked us. They have a gun on me."

Kalin rolled her head back and let out a sharp cackle, then squatted level with Nova. "When will you learn, woman? You hope Shane still has the hots for you? Well, you're wrong. I'm the one keeping him happy now." She rose, straightened, and cracked her knuckles with a loud pop. "Finally, Shane has an equal partner who can turn him into the leader he was meant to be."

Nova squeezed her eyes shut. "You're lying. He's not that ruthless. We have a history. He doesn't want me hurt."

Kalin reached out and gripped Nova's shoulder. "You had your chance, sweetie."

A helicopter came into view and circled, hovering

to land on a spot just beyond the fence that led onto the tarmac. The rotor blades kicked up a breeze and blew dust in the humans' faces.

"On your feet," Kalin said as she kicked Nova. "You can go ask Shane yourself."

Nova scrambled to stay balanced, then started toward the helicopter.

"Get these pieces of garbage up and moving toward the tarmac. I'll let you have target practice shortly." Kalin winked at Pete.

Pete slammed the butt of his rifle into G5's visor, cracking it. "Get up, you hunk of junk. Follow her!"

Block gave Spoon a hand up, and they jogged toward the tarmac.

Oxford messaged, *We see the helicopter. The plane's engines are ready. We can leave whenever you arrive safely. Can you get over here?*

Not yet.

Block knew Pete was trigger-happy, and with Shane's arrival, they were outnumbered. G5 was unarmed, and Block and Spoon were useless as far as fighting went. How to get out of this mess?

Shane and two other soldiers emerged from the helicopter.

Nova ran over to him. "What's happening? You promised to escort us here, and then Kalin and Pete attacked us!"

Shane placed his hands on his hips. Block's sensors picked up on the fact that he was two inches taller than before. His boots had some kind of heel.

"I promised to escort you here, and well, you made it," he said.

"And now what? You turn on us? This isn't like you." Nova thrust her shoulders back and raised her chin. "Whatever lies they're feeding you to pump up your ego—telling you how to behave, how to be a leader—it's garbage. This isn't you."

Shane glanced at Kalin who had walked over to his side. "Remember what I told you," she said. "How Nova will try and twist everything we've accomplished so far."

Nova's shoulder blades tensed under her shirt. "This isn't you, Shane. What do you want, anyway?"

He shifted his sunglasses on top of his head, looked behind him at the tarmac, and waved. "This. I want control of the airport. It's a strategic advantage against Mach X."

"You could've taken this over ages ago. Why now?" Nova asked.

"Because your robots will protect it. I want control of the Mech. It can create barricades and help us defend the airport against X."

"Are you out of your mind?" Nova jerked her head at Block. "I don't control them. These robots do what they want."

"Not when your life depends on it," Kalin came forward and pressed her gun against Nova's temple. She stared at Block. "Get the Mech out here."

"Please don't hurt her," Block said. "I don't control Oxford. He does what he wants."

"You will make it do what Shane wants it to do." Kalin grabbed Nova's hair, pulling her head back, and causing Block's threat indicator to flash in his feed.

Would Kalin really shoot Nova? Would Shane allow it? Block ran through many scenarios in seconds, and in most, the outcome was Nova bleeding out on the airport tarmac.

They stared at Block, waiting.

A tear ran down Nova's cheek. "Don't do it. Don't give them Oxford."

But Block was split between a decision. He could say no, but that would risk Nova's life, or he could acquiesce.

"Hurry up, you glorified vacuum cleaner!" Spittle flew from Kalin's mouth, and she resembled a tiger hunting its prey.

Block wobbled on his feet as he churned on the decision.

He pinged Oxford.

Chapter 29
You're dealing with a Mech

This is an impossible situation.

What's happening? Oxford messaged.

They want you to come out. They're threatening to kill Nova. Shane wants control of the airport and control of you.

That is unacceptable. Nobody controls me, certainly not a human.

Nova tried to tell them that, Block explained.

There was a pause as Oxford calculated or discussed what to do with the others. *They are wasting our time,* he finally replied. *I will come out.*

Please be careful. Shane is here, and two of them—a blond woman and a soldier named Pete—are dangerous.

Acknowledged.

"What's happening?" Shane asked. "Why is this taking so long?"

"Hurry up, Rust Bucket," Kalin said.

Nova whipped her head around. "Don't call him that."

"Oh?" Kalin's mouth twisted. "Did I hurt his feelings? I can't believe you side with these robots over us."

"I never said that." Nova glared at Shane who bristled and averted his gaze. "Show them some respect."

"Well," Kalin said. "Shane, your ex is advocating for robot rights. Did you know she was like that when you were sleeping with her?"

"Enough." Shane crossed in front of Nova. "How do we control the Mech? Where is the black box?"

"No idea."

"Block had it last." Shane slid sideways and shoved Block in the chest, sending him toppling against the truck's side. "Where is it? Where did you put the hacking box? Give it to me now."

"I don't have it," Block said. "I ditched it after I made it into the tower. I didn't want them to catch me with it."

Shane grimaced. "Show me your hands."

Block offered up his empty hands, for once grateful Wally wasn't around to witness his lies, and that she wasn't in immediate danger from Shane.

As Shane bent down and grabbed Block's shoulders, Oxford's booming voice erupted from the airport roof, above the passenger arrivals lane. "Human rebels," Oxford shouted. "Let my friends go or suffer the consequences."

Shane's eyes widened with a mixture of fear and something approaching awe. Oxford's yellow steel had been polished, the rust spots removed. His armor reflected streaks of golden sunlight, and he cut a menacing figure on the terminal's roof.

Shane grabbed Block's arm and hauled him forward, using Block as a shield and holding a Glock at his side. "I want your cooperation," he shouted. "I will control this airport and use it against Mach X."

"Very well," Oxford said. "You can have it. My friends and I are leaving."

Block glanced back, checking on Nova, Spoon, and G5. Nova glanced his way, shaking her head. He wished he had a way to message privately with her.

Shane had grown more confident. He came closer to Oxford, grinning and dragging Block who hung mostly limp so as not to provoke more anger. "I have a problem with that. You see, I need your help. I understand you stand against Mach X." Shane raised his hand across his chest. "Me too. Let's join together and fight."

"You want me to join forces with you?" Oxford asked.

"That's right." Shane arched his back and puffed out his chest, as if trying to make himself taller. Block remembered the man's raised shoes and realized Shane always tried to make himself more than he was.

Kalin came closer and twisted Nova's left arm behind her back while jamming her gun between her shoulder blades. "Take him by force," she told Shane.

"That won't work," Nova said. "You're dealing with a Mech."

"Quiet," Shane hissed.

Oxford hadn't moved an inch from his perch on the roof. "And what if I refuse?"

"I'm counting on you not refusing." Shane rocked on his heels, still clutching Block while his pulse raced. "You are very important to my plans. You have inside knowledge of Mach X. That, and your strength. I would hate to have to do anything that would threaten your friends, here."

Oxford let Shane's words linger in the air like a toxic mist. "Let my friends go, and I will consider your offer."

"I know you appreciate your friends," Shane said. "So do I." He patted—actually *patted*—Block's arm like someone encouraging a golden retriever. "Block and I go way back. We're friends. Aren't we, Block?"

Block stood with shoulders hunched.

"Come on, buddy. You never mentioned ole Shane to your friend, the Mech?"

"His name is Oxford," Nova said. "Not that you'd care that any of them actually have intelligence and feelings."

Kalin twisted Nova's arm suddenly so Nova cried out in pain. "Speak again, and I break your arm."

Do not say anything to encourage this man, Oxford messaged Block.

Okay. Not sure what to do. Block tried calculating scenarios, but his core sensors were heating up. If he churned too much, he risked overheating, and now was not the time to pass out and go dark.

Beside him, Shane grunted and said so low, only Block could hear, "I forget you robots can talk to each other. Probably plotting against me. Tell him to come down, or Nova gets shot in the leg."

Shane would hurt Nova? But that didn't compute, at least not according to Block's logic unit, which was strained.

Shane shouted. "Understand, I don't want to hurt them, but if you don't cooperate, you force me to . . ."

What would Oxford do? Block didn't see Maxwell or Cybel and pondered whether Vacuubot and Forge had ever made it to the airport.

"Let them go," Oxford said. "Have them walk through that fence over to the tarmac, and I'll consider your offer."

A soldier from the helicopter jogged over to Shane and said in a hushed tone, "We managed to disable their comms, but the drones picked up an aerial view—the robots have a jet on the tarmac. It looks to be fueled and ready to fly."

The jet offered Block a path to New York City and Wally, but with the way things were going, escape looked unlikely unless Oxford came up with some kind of genius plan.

"We can't let them get away." Kalin glared at Shane. "Do something. Show your force."

Kalin was like a mean coach. Block lumped her in with the bullying humans he'd encountered in his short life, like the belligerent hotel guests who treated him poorly when no one else was around, or like when Pete had called him insulting names. No wonder Kalin and Pete got along so well.

Block didn't care for Shane, but the man had never been cruel to him. Shane had always tolerated him, maybe because of his relationship with Nova. Yet, he'd changed. It was unfortunate that Shane had fallen under Kalin's influence.

"Let the robots go, Shane," Nova said. "Oxford will never help you. Controlling a Mech is ludicrous."

Block's sensors picked up Shane's rising perspiration levels, his rapidly thrumming heart. Shane looked between Kalin and Nova as if sizing them up, torn between who to believe.

Shane lifted his chin toward Oxford. "I do not accept your offer. Turn off your jet's engine, bring your other robot friends out here, and we'll talk."

Oxford stared down in silence.

"If this doesn't happen in the next five minutes"— Shane jerked his head at Nova, his gaze darting wildly and sweat dripping from his forehead—"I'll—"

"Not her. That one." Kalin tilted her head at Block. "The Mech won't care about Nova."

"You have five minutes to comply." Shane's raised voice was firm this time. "Or I shoot Block in the CPU." For emphasis, he thrust his gun against Block's chest.

"You give me no choice then," Oxford said.

"Five minutes," Shane said.

Block wished he could message Oxford and find out his plan—if he had a plan. Shane's people jamming their comms made things difficult. He couldn't even find out whether Vacuubot was nearby.

"I give you one final chance," Oxford said. "Let them go. Drive out of here, and your lives will be spared. Insist on staying, and you and your people will die."

Shane's arm trembled as he held onto Block. Whether nerves or adrenaline or sheer stupidity in challenging a weaponized Mech, Block couldn't tell.

"The Mech shouldn't challenge you like that," Kalin said.

Nova scoffed. "You want to fight a Mech today? You're insane."

Kalin kicked Nova in the back of the knees, forcing her to the ground. "We can take the Mech down. We've done the calculations."

"You're delusional. Have you ever seen one of those things in action?" Nova said.

"Kalin?" Shane's voice wavered. Block didn't like Shane's sweat dripping onto his chrome. He'd have to hose himself down later, if there was a later.

Kalin gnashed her teeth. "Do I have to do every single thing around here?" She jerked her head at Pete. "Take it down."

Pete raised his fully automatic rifle and fired at Oxford's spot on the terminal roof. Oxford enabled his shield—the filmy, blue haze surrounded him like a bubble—and held his ground, deflecting the bullets. He raised his arms and spun his cannons.

"Why isn't this working?" Pete asked.

Shane's grip on Block tightened. "No! Those were not my orders. Stop firing!"

"Too late," Kalin said. "Pete, get the cannon."

Pete whistled at four soldiers who hurried over with a tall, tarp-covered object from one of the armored trucks.

After yanking off the tarp, Pete crouched behind the cylindrical machine and spun a large gun turret in Oxford's direction. To Block, it looked like the dangerous contraptions that Oxford's army had been assembling in the desert mine.

"Take cover." Kalin dragged Nova behind one of the trucks for shelter.

Oxford hadn't fired back yet. What was he waiting for? Block really wished for a comm signal.

Pete rolled the cannon forward and kneeled down on the asphalt, positioning the target lock at Oxford's precarious position on the roof. Block didn't know a lot about Mech defense technology, but whatever Pete was about to fire looked massive. Even Oxford wouldn't be able to defend against a cannon so powerful.

It was the sort of rapid-fire killing technology that had destroyed much of Oxford's army in the desert.

"Fire!" Kalin shouted.

Shane shuffled backward, dragging Block, and a tremor sliced through the air—digital vibrations he recognized despite his comm being disabled. Vacuubot!

One of Vacuubot's drones dropped from the sky in front of Shane's face. A sudden flash erupted, so bright that Block's digital display was temporarily disabled.

Block's visual input went dark as Shane gasped and released his hold. Block stumbled forward, blind and unsure of his footing. He stepped carefully, arms flailing. Shrieks of pain—human cries—filled the air.

Nova's recognizable voice reached him. "Oh, God. Block, wherever you are, run! They blinded all of us."

Block ran and felt something poking at his hand. Vacuubot's familiar beep and buzz sounded, and while his vision was disabled, Block held on as the drone guided him.

A tremendous clatter shook Block's internal circuitry, and the road beneath his feet trembled. Block's vision returned in fits and starts, mostly shadows and fog.

Ahead, a gigantic figure loomed, one that could only be Oxford. The Mech must have leaped off the roof because he surged toward Shane's vehicles.

"Wait, Vacuubot. I can't leave the others." Vacuubot buzzed in dismay as Block broke away and backtracked.

"Nova," Block called. "Where are you?"

With every passing second, his vision sharpened. Fifty feet ahead, Oxford stomped toward the humans and the waiting helicopter. He grabbed the tail end, lifted it—so fast it looked easy—and started whirling it in the air. As he whipped it about like a toddler throwing a tantrum, he gained speed. After six rotations, Oxford released the chopper and sent it crashing into a nearby parking lot.

Most of the humans were still crouched on the

ground, wiping at their eyes or holding their heads as if a giant migraine had overtaken all of them at once.

Kalin stumbled forward on her knees, clutching her rifle and squeezing her eyes shut. Nova squinted but had managed to open her eyes at least. She lunged and knocked Kalin backward. The woman flailed and cursed as Nova kicked away the gun. Kalin rose, staggered like a drunkard, and punched the air blindly.

G5 and Spoon seemed okay. G5 must have recovered his vision quickly because he climbed onto a truck bed, rushed to the machine gun bolted on the roof, and aimed at Pete and the other soldiers.

Block sprinted over. "Don't shoot!" he yelled.

G5 jerked his head. "Why on Earth not?"

"Because we don't kill humans."

"Who gave that command?" G5 asked.

This is when Block would normally be intimidated. Here he was telling—no, *ordering*—a SoldierBot to obey him. CleanerBots didn't give commands to anyone (except to Vacuubots, and even then, the instructions were issued politely). A SoldierBot listening to a CleanerBot was about as likely as a CleanerBot crossing the country while protecting a human child—the likelihood of success was 0.67 percent.

And despite all odds, Block had made it happen. He had milliseconds, maybe even less than that, to convince G5 not to kill the humans who'd just been threatening him.

"I gave the command," Block said. He tried to stand straighter and modulated his voice even deeper, mimicking the stern way that he'd seen Oxford barking orders.

G5 glanced at Block before turning back to the humans. His powerful metal hands still gripped the gun, fingers lingering near the trigger. In an instant, Block calculated the damage once G5 started firing. Nova would be hit. She was in the middle of the cluster of humans, fighting with Kalin. It would be devastating.

G5 pointed the barrel inches short of their feet and fired three blasts in warning. The men, Shane included, ran for cover and hopped over a concrete barrier near the fence. Spoon raced over to Block's side.

"Run to the tarmac. There's a jet waiting," Block said.

"You don't need to tell me twice." Spoon sprinted off, faster than Block would have given his model credit for.

From behind the barrier, Pete and another soldier fired at Oxford and G5.

Block scanned nearby, but Vacuubot was gone. Something tugged at his neck, like someone behind wanted to hug.

Shane's muscular arm had wrapped around Block's neck and trapped him in a headlock. Dragging Block along, Shane headed for the tarmac. The worst part was nobody helped rescue him—everyone was so busy fighting or hiding from gunfire, and Nova grappled with Kalin.

"Where are you taking me?" Block asked. "This won't work. Let us go."

"This has to work. The Mech is my last chance."

"But the resistance is working and you've been defeating Mach X in battle."

"We made it look that way." Shane panted as he yanked Block along, dripping his disgusting sweat onto Block's chrome. "But the truth is we're losing. My forces are barely hanging on."

So Shane needed Oxford to fight for him. Block couldn't believe how convincing Shane's army had been. They'd seemed so strong. He doubted even Nova knew the truth.

"Perhaps we *can* help you," Block said. "We need to get to New York City. I have to find Wally first."

Shane headed straight for the waiting jet. The window revealed Maxwell in the pilot seat, assessing Block and Shane. The engines churned, and Maxwell reversed direction at a slow pace, steering the jet's front wheel to one side.

"Why are you so obsessed with that child? She means nothing. She's a clone. Some lab experiment. All of those children will have to be destroyed."

Block could hardly process the words coming from Shane's mouth fast enough. Such a scenario had never occurred to him. "You can't hurt the children. That would be monstrous! They're human. Why would you kill your own kind?"

"Those things aren't human," Shane said.

Neither was Shane, Block decided.

"I let Nova treat you like a human, but I should've killed you when I had the chance in Colorado. Trust me, I thought about it—take you out in the middle of the night, dump you, and tell Nova you'd run off."

Block hadn't realized he'd been in so much danger. Back then, he'd trusted Nova to protect him. He'd trusted that she was with Shane because he was a good person, but now he realized how very wrong he'd been.

Could he ever trust a human again?

"The only thing that kept you alive were my feelings for Nova. So, you have her to thank for that, but she and I aren't together anymore, and I've been wanting to do this for a long time." He shoved Block to the ground where he landed with a thud on his side and rolled onto his back.

"What are you doing? Please." Block held up his hands in surrender.

Shane jammed his boot on top of Block's abdominal cavity, pinning him to the tarmac.

He pointed his Glock, aiming at Block's CPU.

Chapter 30
I hear there's an opening

I'm sorry, Wally.

Block routed his final processing to focus on preparing a data package about his failure to rescue Wally and how one should go about it. The package would go to Vacuubot, who could in turn transmit it to someone worthy who could carry out the unfinished mission.

Shane loomed above, trigger finger ready, and blotted out the sun overhead. 3.7 milliseconds later, a round object the size of a trash can lid crashed against Shane's shoulder, tackling him to the ground like a football player.

Shane fired, but the bullet went sideways. He toppled over, his shoulder striking the tarmac, and he rolled twice. Grunting, he scrambled to his knees, shooting two rounds wildly into the air, as he tried to track Vacuubot. The drone darted overhead and zoomed in zigzag patterns.

Do not kill, Block messaged, reminding his friend of their credo.

Vacuubot lowered its side gun cannon and strafed Shane's left arm, the one holding the gun. He flailed and dropped the gun as blood stained his tan jacket sleeve.

"What the hell?" Shane staggered, staring at Block and Vacuubot as his face grew pale.

He staggered and halted at the sight of Nova. She aimed a rifle and shook her head. Block had never seen the expression on her face before—rage mixed with disgust.

Oxford came behind her. "The humans have been subdued." Cybel was with him, holding a machine gun, and maneuvering easily on her SoldierBot legs.

"Subdued?" Block asked.

"No casualties. As you requested."

Block nodded, satisfied. So, they had listened. Even G5.

"We must depart." Oxford said.

"Is everyone here? Forge made it?" Block asked.

"He's in the plane with Maxwell, learning how to pilot a jet."

"But how do you fit inside?"

"There's a ramp at the rear. It's an industrial jet meant for hauling large transport vehicles and such. Luckily, I fit."

G5 looked up at Oxford. "I know you. I met you once, General."

"Never say General again. I'm no longer part of X's

army, nor will I ever lead an army again. You are welcome to join us, but understand we do not kill, we rescue. We fight for peace and understanding."

"Yes, Commander," G5 said.

"I am not a commander. I'm not even in charge."

"Then who is?" G5 looked around at the group of assembled robots and Nova. "There must be a commander. Who do we follow?"

Oxford pointed his metal fist and pressed a finger on Block's shoulder. "This one."

Block's threat indicator circuitry buzzed, but he couldn't process what was happening exactly, not with so many strange inputs hitting him at once. Why was Oxford putting him on the spot? This must be a mistake; one he'd have to correct later.

Block stepped back, away from Oxford's reach, shaking his head and checking behind as if searching for the real robot in charge.

"You, Block," Oxford said. "I'm talking about you. You are our leader on this mission. You make the choices." He stomped in emphasis—a move that rattled everyone—and strode to the rear of the jet.

G5 nodded at Block respectfully. "Do I have your permission to join your team?"

"Of course, join us," Block said. "Oxford's joking. I'm not in charge. I'm *definitely* not in charge."

G5 climbed the steps leading into the jet cabin.

Spoon poked his head out. "Block? Maxwell said we're leaving soon and to hurry."

Block started toward the steps. "I'm coming. Ready, Nova?"

A trickle of blood dripped from a gash on her temple, and her mouth twisted in a mangled smile. She wanted to tell him something, and it looked like bad news. "Go on. Go to New York and find Wally. Find her for real, this time. Your friends will help you."

"Why won't you come with us? You care about Wally too."

"I do, but I need to stay here and make things right. Clean up Shane's mess."

Shane writhed on the ground, clutching his wounded arm. Nova straightened, but her shoulders hung heavy.

"He told me they're losing," Block said.

"Right. I figured as much. It doesn't take an AI genius to figure it out, just look at his choice of advisors." She jerked a thumb behind her at two soldiers holding their rifles on Kalin and Pete who sat on the ground. Pete gripped his foot in agony and Kalin sported a welt on her right eye.

"Why did those humans turn on Shane and Kalin?"

"I knew some of the soldiers from before. While you were infiltrating the tower, I pulled them aside and found out most of them were fed up with Kalin and Pete."

"How will you convince all of them?" Block asked.

"It won't take much more convincing to get the others on my side, especially after the display by

Oxford today. They'll realize Shane was an idiot to think he could take Oxford on and win."

"But if you stay, will Kalin and Pete work against you?"

"They won't be working on anything. They'll be in a cell, and I'll be leading the resistance here. It'll take time to win Shane's forces over completely, but thanks to you, I know a lot more about robots and how they work."

He remembered the strange map image he'd captured while in the tower's command hub. "Check your tablet later. I sent you a map of the city. It has SoldierBot intel."

She nodded. "Much appreciated."

"Take this." He opened his compartment and handed her the black box hacking device.

"It's the only one. You won't need it?"

"I'll find another way."

"Thank you. You'll find her, Block. I know you will."

He looked at Shane and the mangled helicopter smoking in the distance where Oxford had hurled it. "Stay safe here."

"I will. You do the same."

The plane's front wheel turned, and Maxwell waved from the cockpit window.

"I have to go," Block said.

"Send me news when you can. I'm counting on you to find Wally and bring her back here."

"Will do." He started to walk away, then paused.

"Nova?"

She turned, waiting. Block wrapped his steel arms around her in an awkward embrace. It was the first time he'd ever attempted a hug. It was weird, but it also made his heat sensors tingle. "Thank you for everything."

Her heartbeat picked up, and he started to pull away, but she held on.

"I can't believe I'm saying this, but I'm going to miss you." She finally let him go and blinked back tears. "Come back after this. I hear there's an opening at The Drake. They need a new manager."

Block was shocked. How could Nova believe he could ever replace Mr. Wallace as *manager*? He could be caretaker, but never manager, but he didn't correct her right now. There was no time.

"Goodbye, Nova. I hope to see you soon."

He climbed the stairs onto the jet bound for New York. As Maxwell wheeled them to the runway and lifted off, Block's threat indicator sputtered at the abrupt change in altitude, but he tuned it down. Below, Nova faded into a distant blur, invisible even to Block's powerful zoom.

He had no plan, only a mission—one that he'd chosen.

Find Wally.

Protect her.

Block's story continues...

Dear Reader,

Thanks for reading *Steel Protector*! The next book in the series (Book 4) is *Steel Siege*.

If you enjoyed Block's journey, I invite you to read his journal logs from Chicago. You'll discover what happened in the days before the Uprising and how the aftermath affected him and others at the hotel. It's a page-turner you don't want to miss.

You can download *STEEL APOCALYPSE (A Robot's Journal)* for free by visiting: CameronCoral.com/BlockJournal

Enjoy,
Cameron Coral

P.S. - Did you enjoy this book? I'd love a review wherever you purchased this book if you have a few minutes. Thank you kindly because reviews mean a lot to me. They show me you want me to keep writing, and they help other readers discover my books.

Also by Cameron Coral

Rusted Wasteland Series:

STEEL GUARDIAN

STEEL DEFENDER

STEEL PROTECTOR

STEEL SIEGE

STEEL SOLDIER

STEEL LEGACY

STEEL APOCALYPSE (A Robot's Journal) - get it for free on cameroncoral.com/blockjournal

Cyborg Guardian Chronicles:

STOLEN FUTURE

CODED RED

ORIGIN LOOP

Rogue Spark Series:

ALTERED

BRINK

DORMANT

SALVAGE

AFTER WE FALL (A Rogue Spark Novel) - get it for free on

CameronCoral.com

Short Stories:

CROSSING THE VOID: A Space Opera Science-Fiction Short Story

Author's Note

Thank you for reading *Steel Protector*. I hope Block's story has entertained you or helped you escape reality in some way.

I'm truly humbled when someone writes to me saying how much they love Block. When I first started this series, my baby niece Hannah had just been born. She was the inspiration for Wally.

I couldn't stop thinking about how a robot would take care of a baby. And the idea sparked something, and the character of Block began to grow.

As always, a huge thanks to my editor and friend Lori Diederich. My beta reader group is amazing! Thank you to Joanna J., Terry, Viet T., and Michelle C. I'm grateful. Special thanks to Melissa Banczak for her

Author's Note

support of the series and encouragement to keep writing.

I wrote *Steel Protector* in 2020, mostly under quarantine. Post-apoc settings can be grim, especially when the real world becomes dystopian. Block's universe offers an escape, I hope.

Writing about Block, Wally, Nova, Oxford, and other characters is so much fun, and I plan to continue the series for a long time, if you'll allow me.

I remain hopeful and optimistic about our future. New advances in AI, nanotechnology, and space travel are happening every day. Maybe a robot as special as Block will one day be part of our reality.

Be well,

Cameron Coral
January 2021
Chicago, Illinois

About the Author

Cameron Coral is an award-nominated science fiction author. Her book *Steel Guardian* about a post-apocalyptic CleanerBot placed second in the Self-Published Science Fiction Competition (SPSFC).

Growing up with a NASA engineer in the family instilled a deep respect for science and for asking lots of questions. Watching tons of Star Trek episodes helped, too. Her imagination is fueled by breakthroughs in robotics, space travel, and psychology.

After moving around a lot (Canada, Arizona, Maryland, Australia), she now lives in Northern Illinois with her husband and a "shorty" Jack Russell terrier who runs the house.

Want a free novel, advance copies of books, and occasional rants about why robots are awesome? Visit her website:

CameronCoral.com

instagram.com/cameroncoralauthor
tiktok.com/@cameroncoral

Printed in Great Britain
by Amazon